MAX
The
DETECTIVE CAT

The
PHANTOM
PORTRAIT

MAX

The
DETECTIVE CAT

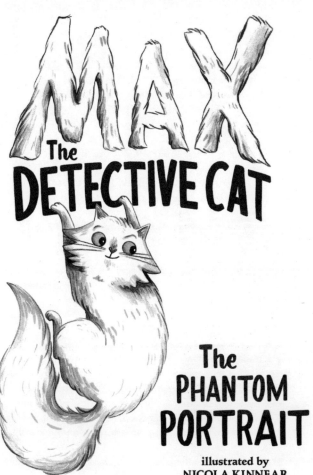

The
PHANTOM
PORTRAIT

illustrated by
NICOLA KINNEAR

Sarah Todd Taylor

nosy
crow

First published 2018 by Nosy Crow Ltd
The Crow's Nest, 14 Baden Place, Crosby Row
London SE1 1YW
www.nosycrow.com

ISBN: 978 1 78800 052 9

Nosy Crow and associated logos are trademarks
and/or registered trademarks of Nosy Crow Ltd

A CIP catalogue record for this book will be available from the British Library

Printed and bound in Great Britain by Clays Ltd, Elcograf S.p.A.

Papers used by Nosy Crow are made from wood grown in
sustainable forests.

1 3 5 7 9 10 8 6 4 2

CHAPTER 1
The Great Furigo

Maximilian peered over the top of Sylvia's bag and miaowed his "can I come out now?" miaow.

"Not yet, old thing," hissed Sylvia. "Wait till the lights go down."

Maximilian grumbled a little. Being crammed into Sylvia's handbag, which was stuffed with lip glosses, mirrors and tram tickets, was not the best thing for his fur. He was sure that his wonderful tail would be most out of sorts by the time he was permitted to climb on to

Sylvia's lap. Still, he had not wished to miss this evening. For one week only "the Great Furigo" was performing his mind-bending illusions at the Oswald Theatre, and Maximilian had been as eager as Sylvia and Agnes to see the tricks that had been astounding all of London. Monsieur Lavroche had arranged for the entire Theatre Royal company to go to the magician's last night as a treat, and they had spoken of little else for weeks.

The lights dipped and Sylvia tickled the top of Maximilian's head. He sneaked out of the bag, padded around on her lap till she hissed at him to keep still and then settled down to watch the show.

And what a show it was! The Great Furigo lived up to his name. He produced rabbits and bunches of flowers from his gleaming top hat. His charming assistant, decked in feathers and spangles, was cut in half in front of the audience's astonished eyes and then magically reassembled. The tip of Maximilian's tail tingled as he tried to work out how each trick was done. He wished very much that Oscar was here, and he could not wait to get back to the Theatre Royal and talk it all over with his old friend.

During the interval Sylvia sneaked him titbits from her ice cream. Agnes was gushing over the last illusion, where Furigo had made his assistant hover in mid-air while he passed hoops around her.

"It's just a trick, Agnes. A very clever one, but still a trick," Sylvia said airily, licking the last of her ice cream from the spoon and ignoring Maximilian's "I could possibly manage just a little more" miaow.

"Well, how did he do it then? Answer me *that*, miss clever clogs," Agnes retorted. "I think it's magic!"

Sylvia tickled the top of Maximilian's head. "You could tell us, couldn't you, Max?" she said. "I bet you've got it all figured out already."

The auditorium filled up once more and Furigo walked on to the stage in front of the theatre's blood-red curtain.

"And now, ladies and gentlemen, for the grand finale of this evening's entertainment," he said. "Let us take you on a journey of the imagination, to a world where anything is possible." He waved a hand in a peculiar twisting gesture, all five fingers pointing to the ceiling, and the curtain flew up to reveal a moonlit graveyard. In a tree at the back of the stage an owl hooted.

"Leave the theatre now if you are of a nervous disposition," Furigo continued. "For tonight we are going to attempt the impossible. We are going to summon and capture a *ghost*."

At this last word the audience gasped. Agnes clutched Sylvia's arm so hard that she jumped in alarm and Maximilian had to dig his claws in to prevent himself from being pitched forwards on to the floor of the theatre.

The magician drew close to one of the

gravestones. Leaning towards the stone he reached out his arms, his fingers spread wide. Slowly he began to draw his hands back as if beckoning something out of the grave and within seconds smoke began to rise from the stage.

Sylvia snorted. "A simple trick," she hissed. "You just need a little hot water to run on to some ice. We used that one in the fairy ballet last season."

Agnes pinched her. "Shush! You're ruining it."

"Really, Agnes, you're awfully foolish. It's just a tr..." Sylvia's voice trailed away. Up on the stage something was rising from the gravestone: a shimmering figure in white. The music from the orchestra pit grew louder and louder. The figure swayed from side to side, rose into the air and began to float towards the audience, skeletal hands clawing at the air. A rasping screech filled the theatre, followed by deep, wailing moans. Maximilian glanced at Agnes, who had slunk down in her seat and covered her face with her

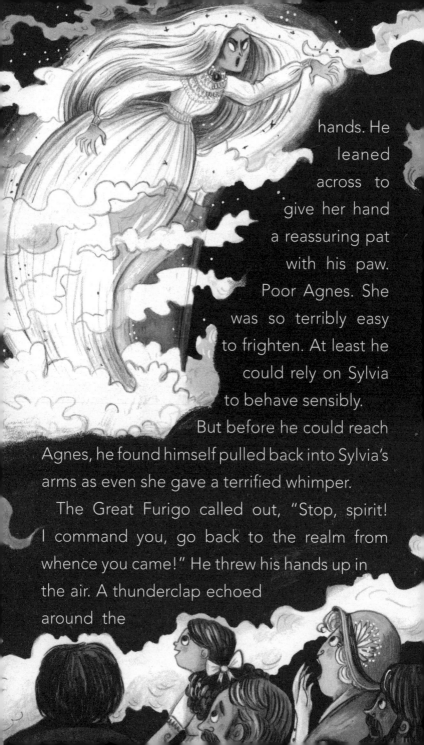

hands. He leaned across to give her hand a reassuring pat with his paw. Poor Agnes. She was so terribly easy to frighten. At least he could rely on Sylvia to behave sensibly.

But before he could reach Agnes, he found himself pulled back into Sylvia's arms as even she gave a terrified whimper.

The Great Furigo called out, "Stop, spirit! I command you, go back to the realm from whence you came!" He threw his hands up in the air. A thunderclap echoed around the theatre. A flash lit up the stage and the spirit was gone.

There was a moment's silence, then the entire theatre erupted in applause.

Back at the Theatre Royal, Monsieur Lavroche had arranged for refreshments to be laid on. Maximilian perched on the stage, eyes closed, as the theatre company milled around him, enjoying a lavish buffet and chattering about how wonderful the show had been. In his head Maximilian waved a paw as Sylvia spun into the air and vanished. The audience applauded and, with a flick of his tail, there was a flash of light and—

"Max, old thing, out of the way. I almost tripped over you," muttered Agnes, her mouth full of sausage roll. Maximilian shook a flurry of crumbs off his tail and tutted. It was so like a human to complain that it was *he* who was in the way. He gave her his "perhaps you should watch where you are going" miaow, but Agnes had dashed over to join the crowd gathering around Monsieur Lavroche. Maximilian saw Mrs Garland, the theatre's costume mistress, chatting with Miss Julier, the musical director. Monsieur Lavroche picked up a glass and tapped it with a silver pastry fork, making it ring out in the echoing space of the auditorium. The company fell silent and waited. Monsieur Lavroche gave a little cough and tugged at his waistcoat.

"As you will know," he began, "our Christmas show will not begin until the second week of December this year, so we have a little time in hand for an additional … project." He reached into his waistcoat pocket and drew out a cream

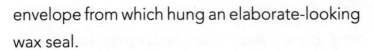

envelope from which hung an elaborate-looking wax seal.

"I have here a letter from Lord Fawley. He has asked us to prepare and perform a unique entertainment for his daughter, Arabella, for the occasion of her eighteenth birthday. We will be his guests for a week at Fawley Castle in Sussex, and will be the main entertainers at the masked birthday ball on Halloween night."

The company broke out into excited chatter. Agnes grasped Sylvia's arm.

"How thrilling," Agnes said. "A masked ball in a castle, and at Halloween. How creepy!"

Sylvia rolled her eyes. "Oh, don't start all that nonsense about ghosts again."

Agnes ignored her. "But think, Sylvia," she breathed, her voice dropping to a low whisper. "An old estate out in the country. There are bound to be towers, maybe even a *dungeon*. Monsieur Lavroche said *Fawley Castle*."

"Every threepenny country house calls itself

a castle nowadays, you ninny," scoffed Sylvia. "I'm sure it will be quite modern and very comfortable."

"And I'm sure it will be cold and draughty and probably haunted," said Agnes. She scooped Maximilian up into her arms and looked deep into his eyes. "You wait! Max will be able to sense it. Animals *know*. It's in their whiskers, isn't it, Max?"

Maximilian gave her a miaow that was intended to convey both deep intelligence and scepticism at the very idea of ghosts. Agnes was getting rather silly about them and she would only be worse once she was in a damp and draughty castle.

Maximilian gave a shudder as an awful thought struck him. There would be no need for him out in the countryside. Monsieur Lavroche would probably want him to stay in the theatre, carrying on his work as Theatre Royal Mouser. Or would he be sent away to the "Cat and

Kitten Kennels" that he had heard of from his friend Oscar, where cats were left by their owners and sometimes never collected? He looked at Agnes and gave out a mournful little "I am coming too, aren't I?" miaow, but she just deposited him on the floor and dragged Sylvia off to quiz Monsieur Lavroche about Fawley Castle, leaving Maximilian on his own in the middle of the stage.

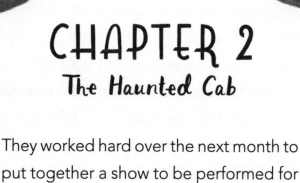

CHAPTER 2
The Haunted Cab

They worked hard over the next month to put together a show to be performed for one night only for Arabella Fawley. At the end of the month the company gathered outside the theatre, where Lord Fawley had instructed twelve cars to collect them for the journey to Sussex. They were surrounded by boxes of costumes and make-up and props, and Mrs Garland ran from case to case, checking that they were securely locked and ticking them off in a small cloisonné notebook.

Maximilian sat by the edge of the road, trying to keep his tail out of the gutter. After much begging from Sylvia and Agnes, Monsieur Lavroche had agreed that Maximilian could come with them, but Maximilian was taking no chances that he might be left behind in all the excitement. Sylvia was inclined to be forgetful and she had already dashed back into the theatre to collect her favourite wrap, her mother-of-pearl hairclips and a book she was halfway through reading.

Maximilian cast an eye up to the roof of the theatre, where Oscar often slept. How he wished that Oscar would come to Sussex with them too. It would be much more fun to be out in the country with his best friend. Oscar told the most entertaining stories in the world, mostly tall tales about how he lost his eye, and Maximilian had been looking forward to exploring the castle with him. Sylvia and Agnes were lovely, of course, but till they learned Cat, conversations would always be a little one-sided.

At twelve fifteen precisely, a smart fleet of liquorice-black cars swept up to the doors of the theatre. Monsieur Lavroche helped Mrs Garland into the first one while the rest of the company dashed to get good seats. Agnes and Sylvia found themselves lucky to have a car to themselves and climbed in, jostling one another for space on the wide leather seat. Maximilian gave out a little "mrow" of annoyance and jumped in after them.

"Sorry, Max," Sylvia said, tickling him behind his ear. "We wouldn't *really* have forgotten you, honest."

Maximilian stuck his chin in the air and looked out of the window. He might decide to forgive them after his afternoon snack, he supposed.

Agnes slid the battered case that held her favourite hat under their seat and, turning to Sylvia, returned to her favourite topic of whether the castle was haunted. Maximilian pressed his face to the window and peered out at the theatre but Oscar did not appear, dashing down the street, his one eye sparkling in the winter sun. Maximilian miaowed a little disappointed miaow and, squeezing himself between Agnes and Sylvia, he dropped his head on to his paws and sighed.

He woke to the sound of Agnes and Sylvia quarrelling. Outside, it was a beautiful night and the shadows of trees, lit by a full moon, flashed by them on each side.

"Please close that window, Agnes!" Sylvia scolded. "It's freezing in here."

Agnes, leaning half out of the window, looked back and pulled a face.

"I want to see the castle," she complained. Her eyes grew large and bright in the moonlight. "It's a full moon. I'll bet the ghosts are all out tonight."

Maximilian miaowed his "that's werewolves" miaow, but Agnes ignored him. He shivered and felt his hair standing on end, not because he was nervous but because he was cold. Agnes was being particularly silly.

"Agnes," began Sylvia, but her voice died away as an eerie scratching broke the silence of the night. Sylvia looked up at the roof of the car and shuddered. For a few moments all was quiet, but then the scratching grew louder. Agnes pulled her head back into the cab and threw herself on to the seat next to Sylvia.

"I told you there were ghosts," she whimpered.

Sylvia clutched her hand and said nothing, but Maximilian could see that even she was frightened. There was another scratch and the car lurched to one side, making both girls scream, and Agnes's hatbox slid out from under the seat and tumbled across the cab. The lid flew off and a dark shadow rolled out. One green orb glinted in the moonlight. Maximilian gasped. It was Oscar!

Agnes screeched. She drew her feet up on to

the seat and grabbed at Sylvia's arm, making Sylvia cry out with pain. Then she kicked out at Oscar. He flinched and leapt out of the way just as the car made a great lurch to the side. Oscar flew to the open window,

landing precariously on the slender door. Maximilian followed, miaowing at Agnes "don't panic" and "it's only Oscar". As the car rounded a corner, Maximilian felt himself falling backwards. He flicked his tail to the side to try to keep his balance, but it was no match for his rather portly bottom and, with a miaow of panic, he and Oscar tumbled out of the car window towards the ground, landing in a rolling muddy heap in the dark. Maximilian saw Sylvia's face at the window, heard his name shouted in alarm on the cold night air, but in seconds they were far away. The fleet of cars rushed past them, throwing dust up into the air, and a few moments later Maximilian and Oscar were alone in the dark as Monsieur Lavroche's company sped on to Fawley Castle.

CHAPTER 3
Noises in the Dark

The three things Maximilian hated most were being hungry, dirty and cold, in precisely that order. At the moment that he and Oscar saw the lights of the final car disappear into the night, he found to his dismay that he was dirty, cold and hungry all at once. His beautiful fluffy tail was covered in mud, a beetle had rudely crawled on to his nose, and his tummy was making the sort of noises that it liked to make when he hadn't had any salmon for over an hour. He stared into

the dark at where the cars had been, and miaowed a "come back!" miaow that echoed around the night.

Beside him, Oscar stretched and sniffed the air. "Vole," he muttered. "A little like mouse, but more of a delicacy."

Maximilian's tummy gave a groan.

"Why didn't they stop?" he wailed.

"Humans are not very good at quick thinking," Oscar said. "They'll be at the castle gates before it occurs

to any of them to stop panicking and simply ask the driver to stop and wait for you. We'll just have to walk."

Maximilian's tummy groaned again. The trees seemed to go on forever and there was no sign of the castle lights. If only Oscar hadn't escaped from the hatbox!

They set off down the road, the shadows creeping around them. When the moon was out, the trees rose above them, their long branches entwining round one another like nests of snakes. When the moon was covered by a passing cloud, the night closed in and all that Maximilian could see was the glinting stars above. He had never noticed before how quiet the night-time was. In London there was always noise, even when the theatre shut its doors for the night. He and Oscar would sit up on the roofs and listen to the bustle of traffic and nightclubs and restaurants far below, the sounds blurring into one comforting buzz of life. Out here, in the dark silence of the night, every tiny sound was amplified. The snap of a twig as a shrew ran over it echoed like a falling tree. The squeak of a mouse shrieked in his ears. Maximilian began to dread the moments when the moonlight disappeared. He walked a little closer to Oscar than usual, glad that his friend was here.

As they neared the top of a hill, a cloud cut across the moon, making the shadows that surrounded them dance. Maximilian jumped as something pale and shimmering swooped down from the trees above and dived into the undergrowth.

"It's just an owl," he told himself, hoping that Oscar had not noticed how jumpy he was getting. It was all Agnes's fault, with that silly talk about ghosts.

Ahead of him, Oscar had paused and was staring into the distance. Maximilian joined him and together they gazed down a tree-lined avenue to a pair of intricately wrought gates rising high above them. Beyond the gates was the shadow of a vast house. Towers twisted into the night sky at either end and lights flickered in dozens of windows. The moonlight settled on the stonework, highlighting great marble lions standing by an archway at the front of the house, and picking out strange carvings set into the roof of monsters screaming and eagles taking flight. It was Fawley Castle.

Maximilian felt his heart leap, followed by his tummy. He was just a few hundred cat leaps away from a bite of supper and a quiet nap. Flicking his tail with joy, he bounded forwards and was halfway down the avenue when a strange sound filled the night, a deep droning like the heavy buzzing of a bee but much, much louder. Maximilian looked back. Oscar was hunkered down, scanning the sky and ready to spring at whatever was about to attack them. Maximilian crouched as well and peered into the night.

The droning grew louder and from behind a low cloud a creature emerged. It had wide wings that glinted in the moonlight and one dazzling eye, flooding the ground below with light.

Maximilian's fur stood on end. He saw Oscar falter and stumble back a little as the creature dived down towards them. The drone became a clattering scream in his ears. The light of its eye blinded him.

And in seconds it had zoomed over them,

leaving a choking stream of smoke in its wake. As it flew beneath the trees the lower branches caught at its wings and a horrible scraping sound ripped through the air. Oscar dashed to Maximilian's side.

"It's a plane!" he cried. "It's just a plane. What a fool, flying so close to the ground. He could have crashed."

Maximilian had never seen a plane, though Sylvia had shown him many newspaper photos of Lady Hawksmere, who was said to be planning to cross the Mediterranean on her own in the spring and who Sylvia thought was the bravest woman on earth. Far away from them, the plane soared over the gates that led to the castle. It tilted, turning gracefully in the air, before zooming out of sight to the east, leaving the night as calm and quiet as it had been only a few moments before. Maximilian padded over to one of the tree branches that had broken off as the wings of the plane scraped underneath them.

"The sound it made when it hit the trees," he murmured. "Do you think it might have been—"

"The sound that we heard in the car?" asked Oscar. "Yes! Of course, that's what the scraping noise on the roof of the cab was – it was the branches of the trees catching the roof."

Maximilian let out a sigh of relief. Every ghost so far was turning out to be something perfectly normal. So much for Agnes and her silly stories!

Feeling much braver, Maximilian let out a "come on then" miaow and set off towards Fawley Castle, shaking all thought of ghosts and creatures in the night from his paws and dashing on towards supper and a nice lie-down.

CHAPTER 4
A Surprise in the Grounds

Fawley Castle, from the outside, looked to be just as Agnes had predicted. It was a great dark building with leaded-glass windows, screeching gargoyles along the guttering, and towers that bent over to peer at the ground in a most alarming way. Maximilian looked up at the roof with its tilting slates and thought it just the place for a midnight walk while listening to one of Oscar's wonderful stories.

They wandered through the grounds, the gravel of the path crunching under-

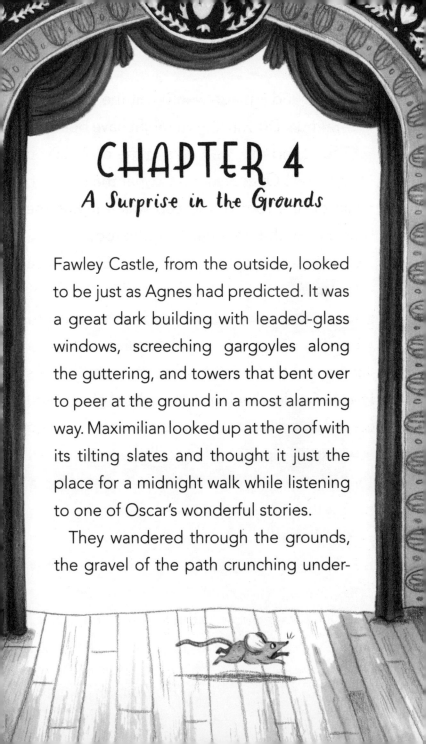

paw. The flowerbeds were surrounded by neat box hedges, and an assortment of trees cut into intricate topiary shapes decorated the lawns.

"What splendid grounds," Oscar said, pausing to sniff at a jasmine flower. "They remind me of the garden where I saved the life of the Lord Chancellor when he was choking on a fishbone."

Maximilian was about to ask how, when something caught his eye. At the end of one of the grand sweeping lawns was a curved building with nine stone pillars and arched windows. On the top was a great glass dome. The tip of Maximilian's tail tingled, the way it did whenever there was a puzzle that he wanted to solve.

He dashed down the lawn towards the building, followed by Oscar. The closer they drew, the surer Maximilian was. From the smart revolving glass doors to the empty frames hung by the window, ready for posters or glamorous photos to be displayed in them, it was clear what this place was.

"How extraordinary," murmured Oscar. "Do you think it really is?" Maximilian saw his friend's glance flick upwards to the roof, where the glass dome bounced starlight back across the lawns.

"There's only one way to find out," said Maximilian.

A few minutes later and they were up on the roof, staring down through the dome.

Maximilian had been right. Below them was a circular space with ten or so rows of seats, upholstered in a velvet so soft it shimmered in the night. On either side of the rather small stage a narrow twisting staircase led to a box just big enough for three or four people. There were swags of velvet hanging from the walls and golden lanterns hung around the room, their etched glass twinkling in the moonlight.

"A theatre!" Oscar gasped. "What an extravagance. It's splendid. Rather small, but splendid."

Maximilian looked at the stage. If this was where the company was to perform, then he suspected that Sylvia would be disappointed once she saw how little space she had to show off her dancing. It certainly was splendid of Lord Fawley to have his own theatre, though. He was about to say so when his tummy, thoroughly sick of being ignored, let out the loudest rumble it could.

"I rather think you should go in and find Sylvia and Agnes," Oscar said.

Maximilian nodded. "What about you?"

Oscar waved a paw. "With this magnificent theatre all to myself and a veritable feast of voles and mice only a whisker away? I shall be quite comfortable."

Maximilian grinned. He was glad to have his old friend with him on this adventure, and with a tiny version of the Theatre Royal to play in they would be quite at home. His tummy gave another warning rumble and he leapt from the roof and headed towards the castle.

CHAPTER 5
The Mystery of the Staircase

Intricately carved, with a border of crescent moons and a brass knocker in the shape of a star, the doors to Fawley Castle were very beautiful.

They were also very shut.

Maximilian pressed his ear to the wood. He could hear muffled laughter and the pop of wine corks. He strained to hear Sylvia's or Agnes's voice. Surely they would not be enjoying a party when he was missing? Maximilian frowned. Why had they not come out to find him?

Still leaning against the castle doors, Maximilian was just pondering whether to try to find an open window, when he felt himself falling forwards. The cold marble of the floor rose to meet him as the door of the castle swung open and he was swept into the hall.

Fawley Castle's entrance hall was a great cavern of a space. Cream stone arches rose to the roof past two sets of galleries, curving over to meet one another high above. Suits of armour lined the lower hall, and paintings and rich tapestries hung on the walls above. High up, suspended from the ceiling by a chain on which crystals shimmered, hung the largest chandelier Maximilian had ever seen, larger even than the one in the Theatre Royal. Maximilian smiled. This was evidently a place of deep feather pillows and comfortable velvet cushions, which was *just* the sort of place of which Maximilian approved.

The floor of the hall was glossy white marble, gleaming bright and very slippery under-paw.

Maximilian clambered to his feet but soon found himself all at sea on the smooth surface and he was appalled to find himself sliding on his bottom the length of the hall and bumping his nose on the bottom of the stairs. Hearing a squeal of laughter behind him, he picked himself up with as much dignity as he could muster and stuck his tail in the air to show that *some cats* did not find that in the slightest bit amusing.

"Poor kitty," said a girl's voice, light and trilling. "I hope he hasn't hurt himself."

Maximilian glanced round, lifting a paw to rub at his bruised nose. He hoped that his whiskers were not bent out of shape. A broad-set middle-aged man with dark bushy hair and wearing a voluminous greatcoat and a hat with what looked like spectacles stretched over the top was standing in the doorway. Beside him stood a thin-faced girl of about eighteen. She wore the same ridiculous hat, but golden curls peeped out from beneath hers. The door

34

behind them swung wide, letting the cold blast into the room.

The man stepped into the hall, put his fingers to his lips and let rip an ear-splitting (and most ungentlemanly) whistle that echoed around the vast space and set Maximilian's hair on end. From a door to the side came a guffaw of laughter and a jovial-looking man with very spindly legs clad in tartan trousers of a most alarming shade of green came bowling out of a brightly lit room, his arms open wide for an embrace.

"Maurice Rorston, my old friend!" the man cried. "It's been an age! Welcome, welcome! Did you come by car or is that ridiculous flying machine of yours tearing up one my lawns? The gardener almost banned me from inviting you."

Ah, thought Maximilian. *So this is who came in the aeroplane. And the man in the alarming tartan must be Lord Fawley, if they are his lawns.*

The bushy-haired man laughed a deep-throated laugh. "My 'ridiculous machine', as you call it, is parked on the East Lawn, well away from the festivities, though I fear I may have trimmed some of the estate's topiary on the way down." He laughed again, although Maximilian could not see what was so very funny.

"And, Bunty, my dear girl," said Lord Fawley to the young girl. "Why, you grow more beautiful every time I see you. You're just in time for dinner. It's a little late, but we waited as we wanted your company."

Bunty put a hand up to pat her hair. "I ... I

haven't time to dress," she said, but Lord Fawley waved her objection aside.

"You look delightful. Arabella has been dying to see you. And I have a surprise treat for you. Now then, do you remember the old theatre that you and Arabella used to pester me to open as children? Well, after months of work cleaning out the cobwebs, and a little building work to make it safe, we have reopened the old place and a troupe from London's Theatre Royal will be here to entertain you all."

An odd silence fell over the pair. Maximilian preened. No doubt they were awestruck at the thought of being entertained by the Theatre Royal company. But when the girl finally spoke it was clear that she had not given the treat even a fleeting thought. She stared at Lord Fawley, her eyes widening. "Goodness, but what about…" Her voice died away as she began to blush a deep pink and motioned vaguely towards the end of the hall. Maximilian glanced over but all he could see was the wide sweeping staircase leading up to a balconied landing.

Lord Fawley laughed. "Oh, my dear girl, don't tell me that you believe all that nonsense."

"But Lady Celine—" Bunty began.

"Will not be bothering us, I assure you."

The young girl bit her lip and glanced again at the staircase. Maximilian felt the tip of his tail tingle. Who was Lady Celine, and why was Bunty so worried about the theatre being used? Maximilian stared at the staircase, half expecting an angry, theatre-hating woman to storm down it and throw them all out, but instead Agnes and Sylvia arrived at the top and dashed down towards him.

"There you are, Max!" cried Sylvia. "We were so worried about you. Trust you to find your own way here, clever old puss."

Maximilian pouted. He was still very disappointed in Sylvia. Why had she not stopped the car and come to get him? He drew himself up in a very dignified manner and began to groom his tail. It was alarmingly grubby from being dragged in the mud and he was painfully aware that he was not looking at all his best, and in front of strangers too. It was most mortifying.

"Oh, don't sulk, old thing," Sylvia said, crouching down to tickle his ears.

Maximilian was debating whether to ignore her or relent and be friends again when the dinner gong rang. All of a sudden the hall seemed full of people as the rest of the theatre company swept past, their feet clattering around Maximilian on the marble floor. Only Mrs Garland noticed him.

"What on earth has made Maximilian so muddy?" she demanded, looking sternly at Sylvia and Agnes. "A bath after dinner, I think."

Maximilian's blood ran cold and he set to his grooming with renewed vigour. Anything was better than a bath!

CHAPTER 6
A Ghostly Sighting

Cats, it seemed, were not welcome in the dining room, at least as far as the staff were concerned. Lord Fawley's butler tried repeatedly to shoo Maximilian out, and a footman went so far as to give him a sly kick as he passed him on the way to the table with a platter full of delicious-smelling salmon. Maximilian was particularly partial to salmon and his tummy was feeling very empty, as he had failed to have either of his usual afternoon snacks.

"Maximilian goes everywhere we go," Sylvia explained to Lord Fawley, beckoning Maximilian to sit by her feet.

Lord Fawley beamed at them amiably. "He reminds me of my grandmother's cat, a wonderful beast called Edgar," he said, and launched into a long story about an old cat that had once belonged to the family. Maximilian only half listened. Lord Fawley's stories were not as interesting as Oscar's.

"... and it took us forever to get it all out of his fur!" Lord Fawley finished. The company burst into obliging laughter.

Maximilian looked around the dining room. It was richly furnished in red velvet wallpaper and hung with ornate mirrors and old family portraits, but from where he sat by Sylvia's feet under the huge dining table that ran the length of the room, all Maximilian could see was a sea of legs. At one end of the table were Lord Fawley's feet, in rich-green dress shoes with silver buckles.

Next to him were the dainty silver slippers of his daughter, Arabella. Arabella had endeared herself to Maximilian by making a great fuss of him when he sneaked into the dining room and secretly feeding him a slice of salmon under the table. She was a very pretty girl of seventeen, with dark, twinkling eyes and glossy black hair cut into a fashionable bob, and she had the most bewitching laugh. She talked to Sylvia and Agnes almost as though they were old friends, promised to show them all over the estate, and begged them to have late-night ghost stories in the library with her and Bunty "just like we did at boarding school".

Maximilian weaved his way between the legs of the theatre company to sit by Bunty, who was asking Monsieur Lavroche question after question about the theatre and all the famous names who had appeared in his shows.

"We are all looking forward to working in Lord Fawley's theatre, of course," Monsieur Lavroche said gallantly. "The finest miniature theatre in England, I'm told."

"It's wonderful!" gushed Arabella. "I can't wait for Saturday. I've wanted a Halloween ball for ages but Papa always said they were ghoulish. I've got the most heavenly dress, all the way from Paris, but I won't tell you what I'm going as, because that would spoil the fun. We're all to wear masks and remove them at midnight, and there's to be a real French orchestra playing on the terrace, and ice sculptures in the rose garden, and fire jugglers around the ornamental lake, a spectacular ghost's galleon, and a firework display…" She took a great gasp as she ran out of breath and then broke into giggles, blushing a pretty pink.

Bunty sneaked a tiny morsel of her beef to Maximilian and winked at him. He purred his thanks and sat attentively in case of any more titbits that Bunty should like to dispose of. Maximilian prided himself on his nose for people who were "good sorts", and Bunty was definitely falling into that category. She "dropped" another morsel down to him and leaned closer to Monsieur Lavroche, so only he and Maximilian could hear what she said next.

"I do hope none of the ladies will be frightened by the story of Lady Celine's ghost," she whispered. "I would be terrified to set foot in that theatre myself."

Maximilian's ears pricked up at this. So Lady Celine was a ghost! But then why was Bunty so worried that she would come down the staircase?

Monsieur Lavroche laughed nervously and tugged at his cravat. "A ghost, you say? Well, no theatre is truly respectable without a ghost. Our own Theatre Royal has one, you know, though I've never seen him myself."

Maximilian rolled his eyes. The humans were really very silly about the theatre ghost. Agnes refused to go into the costume store on her own because she thought she once saw it creeping up on her in the dark. Maximilian suspected the real reason was so she didn't get trapped into helping Mrs Garland with any mending.

"Oh, but Lady Celine is different," Bunty began. Maximilian noticed that although the girl had talked of being terrified, she did not look in the slightest bit afraid. She rather looked as though she was enjoying it all. "It's all to do with her portrait…"

At this moment the footmen came round with the dessert, which was a delicious-looking creamy concoction. Maximilian wondered whether he should go back to Sylvia, who might be persuaded to share hers, but there was something about Bunty's eagerness to tell Monsieur Lavroche about the ghost that made him curious. And what was all this about her portrait?

With the parfait to enjoy, however, Bunty said not a word more, so Maximilian weaved his way back to Sylvia, who did not disappoint.

The talk moved on to the plans for Arabella's party. Monsieur Lavroche described the show that they were devising in her honour and exclaimed at length over how wonderful the costumes would be. Bunty patted the side of her mouth with a napkin and excused herself with a slight headache after the long journey. Maximilian miaowed his "if there is any cream left, I have space for a little more" miaow, but Sylvia was deep in conversation with Agnes, so he went out into the hallway to investigate the curious matter of the staircase.

Taking greater care on the slippery floor this time, he padded over and mounted the stairs. Close up, he could see that the carvings in the wooden panelling that had looked so intricate were hundreds of crescent moons entwining with one another. A row of stars ran along the banister. Maximilian bounded up the stairs, taking the left-hand side where they divided, and soon reached the landing. There was a long gallery that ran round above the hall, lit by lamps set into the walls. At the top of each side of the staircase stood a stone plinth holding a beautiful midnight-blue vase with stars and moons picked out in shimmering gold running round its rim and base.

On the landing above the staircase, behind a stone balustrade, stood a sideboard of polished walnut. It was bare except for a silver candlestick at each end, but above it was a huge portrait stretching high up towards the vaulted ceiling of the hall. It was of a woman in a midnight-blue gown, flecked to look like velvet and spotted with tiny stars. Maximilian could almost feel the weight and softness of the cloth. It pooled in soft waves around the woman's feet. Her dark hair was swept into elaborate coils, secured with a glittering tiara, and her eyes, sapphire blue and piercing, stared down under richly lashed lids. Maximilian glanced around at the other paintings down in the hall. Most of them

were set against elaborate backdrops of country parks or elegant sitting rooms. But there was no background on the portrait of the woman. She was set against a mottled grey and blue canvas, so that she looked almost to be floating in the night sky.

As Maximilian was staring at the portrait, he heard footsteps behind him. He glanced round, but the hall was empty. The clinking sounds of coffee cups and port glasses floated up from the dining room. Maximilian leapt up on to the sideboard, his paws scrabbling a little on its highly polished surface, and scanned the hall, peering into the dark spaces in the galleries. He was the only living soul in the hall but still he could hear footsteps, and not above him but to the side, as though someone were pacing down the gallery. The sound grew closer and Maximilian felt his fur standing on end. He squinted into the shadows but there was no one there, only the "click, click" of the footsteps, growing louder with each step till they seemed to pass by him and die away.

Maximilian let out a tiny miaow, sprang from the sideboard and dashed down the stairs. He hit the marble floor at such speed that his back paws shot forwards between his front paws and he slid the length of the hall again, this time flat on his back, desperately waving his legs in the air and trying to steer with his tail.

"Oh, Max, you are silly!" cried Sylvia, coming from the dining room arm in arm with Agnes. Maximilian spun to a stop at her feet and righted himself, flicking his tail in annoyance. *Really!* Why was it that humans were able to appear the minute a cat was looking his worst?

Lord Fawley chuckled as he passed by and muttered something that sounded like "just like

Grandmother's old cat".

"We'll say goodnight then, Lord Fawley," said Monsieur Lavroche, beaming from ear to ear. "Up bright and early for rehearsals, everyone."

The company groaned good-naturedly. A small army of maids and footmen appeared as if from nowhere to escort them to their rooms.

Arabella walked up with Sylvia and Agnes. At the top of the stairs they paused and Agnes pointed to the portrait of the woman in the blue gown.

"She is so beautiful."

"That's Lady Celine, the wife of the first Lord Fawley, who built the theatre," Arabella said. "He loved his theatre but Lady Celine thought it was common. She hated seeing him waste all his money on it, even selling her precious jewels to pay for an extension on it, so one night she had her revenge."

Arabella's voice had sunk to a whisper and her eyes twinkled with excitement. Agnes and

Sylvia leaned close, their faces agog.

"On the night before the grand opening, when His Lordship had invited half the county down and had bought in theatricals from London to entertain them, Lady Celine crept out in the dead of night and set fire to the theatre. She was caught in the blaze and died. The first Lord Fawley was so heartbroken that he closed the theatre for good."

"How terrible!" shuddered Sylvia.

"That's not the half of it," Arabella said. "The night she died, her most precious tiara disappeared. The Moonrise."

She pointed up to the portrait. On top of the woman's dark curls sat a tiara of crescent moons, each larger than its neighbour. In the centre was a full moon, a single sparkling diamond. Arabella sighed. "It should come to me on my eighteenth birthday, but they say that Lady Celine's ghost took it to protect it from Lord Fawley. It's all nonsense. It probably just got sold with the other jewels. But it's a delicious thought that it's still in the house somewhere, protected by Lady Celine's ghost. Of course, there are some who say that it is too dangerous to open the theatre again, but that's all nonsense too."

"What is?" asked Agnes.

Arabella grinned, but what she said next did not sound very funny. She looked at Agnes, her eyes gleaming with excitement.

"That portrait is meant to bear a family curse," she said. "They say that if the theatre is ever opened again, Lady Celine will come down from it and haunt whoever dares to perform there."

CHAPTER 7
The Fawley Curse

"Well, I agree with Arabella," said Sylvia once she had closed the door to the bedroom that she and Agnes had been given. "It's nonsense. A cursed portrait? Utter piffle."

Agnes flopped down on to the nearest bed and wrapped herself in a warm raspberry wool blanket. She shivered. "What if it's not?"

Maximilian jumped up beside her and nuzzled his soft head against her hand. He was inclined to agree with Sylvia.

Cursed portraits! Humans would believe anything. The story of Lady Celine solved one tiny mystery, however. It explained why Bunty had glanced so nervously towards the staircase. It must have been the portrait she was thinking of.

Sylvia was far more sensible, as usual. "Oh, Agnes, look at the place!" she laughed. "Does it look like a haunted ruin?" She waved her hand around the room. It was beautifully done out in delicate pinks and creams, and someone had left a bunch of violets on each of their bedside tables. The comfortable beds were a far cry from the rather knobbly-looking ancient furniture in the castle hall, and there was even an ample armchair with plump cushions that would, Maximilian thought, be a perfect sleeping spot for a cat who liked such things.

"Well, I'm locking the door every night," Agnes muttered. "I'm not having some ghost after me just because we opened up her silly theatre."

Maximilian rolled his eyes. He left Agnes to

her sulk and padded across the room. A short leap and he was looking out of the leaded-glass window across the lawns of the castle to Lord Fawley's theatre. The moon was out in full and the glass dome glinted in the moonlight. On the top sat a black cat, listening to the sounds of the night.

After breakfast the next day Lord Fawley led the company across the lawn. Monsieur Lavroche was in his element, gushing about what a treat it would be to perform in a genuine miniature theatre. Mrs Garland had taken her notebook out of her tapestry bag and was counting off the boxes that she hoped had been delivered safely. Maximilian wound himself round her ankles, miaowing his "don't worry, nothing will have been forgotten" miaow.

At the door to the theatre Lord Fawley drew from his waistcoat pocket what looked like a silver pencil. He winked at Agnes and pressed a button on the end. With a gentle click three diamond-studded moons spun out of the end and snapped into place.

"It's the secret key," Lord Fawley whispered. "I had it fashioned especially."

Agnes clapped her hands with delight. Lord Fawley turned the key in the lock, swept open

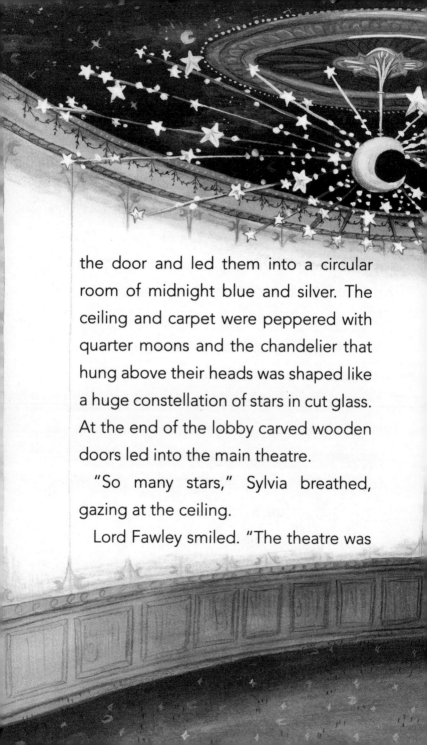

the door and led them into a circular
room of midnight blue and silver. The
ceiling and carpet were peppered with
quarter moons and the chandelier that
hung above their heads was shaped like
a huge constellation of stars in cut glass.
At the end of the lobby carved wooden
doors led into the main theatre.

"So many stars," Sylvia breathed,
gazing at the ceiling.

Lord Fawley smiled. "The theatre was

built over a hundred years ago," he said. "The first Lord Fawley styled it on the night sky in honour of his wife, Lady Celine. Celine is the name of a goddess of the moon. You'll see moons all over the castle if you look carefully."

He led them through to the auditorium where the company explored gleefully, with Agnes squealing with delight over each new discovery. Maximilian saw Sylvia biting her lip at the size of the stage and knew that he had been right to suspect she would find it too small to show off her dancing. Mrs Garland made a beeline for backstage to check on her costumes and props. Miss Julier settled herself into the mini pit at the front of the stage and flexed her arms as if conducting a small orchestra. The men of the chorus took flying leaps over her head to the stage and broke out into an improvised dance. As the laughter of the company filled the space, Maximilian looked upwards to the dome, where Oscar's face peered down over them. He whisked his tail in greeting and went to join his friend.

"Cursed?" Oscar said.

Maximilian nodded. "A haunted portrait, apparently, and a mysterious missing tiara."

"Sounds like just the right atmosphere for a Halloween party," said Oscar. "Did I ever tell you about when I saw the ghost of a pterodactyl on the top of the Natural History Museum?"

Maximilian smiled. If only the humans had Oscar's stories to listen to, Arabella's party would be bound to be a success. He settled down to enjoy another while the theatre company practised below them.

It was about six o'clock when the first fat drops of rain fell on to the roof of the theatre and the early-evening sky began to darken with the threat of a downpour. Maximilian and Oscar hurried down from the roof to take shelter. The doors were ajar and, leaving Oscar enjoying the sight of the rain from the comfort of the porch, Maximilian slipped inside to see the rehearsal in full swing.

Monsieur Lavroche had created a brand-new show in honour of Arabella's birthday, to fit perfectly with the Halloween ball. It was about a young village maiden cursed by a witch, and the ghost of a handsome farmer who helped her break the curse. Agnes was playing the young maiden and the final song was the perfect opportunity for her to show off her lovely singing voice. Sylvia would be dancing the part of the ghostly young farmer, her glossy hair tucked away under a cap and a moustache painted over her top lip.

Everyone except Agnes was up on the stage, where Sylvia was working through how she could do nine pirouettes without falling into the orchestra pit. She had just turned lightly on her toes for the sixth time when the lights of the theatre flickered, making her miss her step. Miss Julier, the company's chorus mistress and choreographer, puckered her brow and tutted at the interruption.

"There must be a storm brewing," she said.

"Unless..." whispered Agnes, her eyes wide.

Sylvia frowned at her. "Oh, don't start that haunting nonsense again, Agnes," she sighed.

The lights flickered on and off again. Sylvia shrugged and resumed her dance, but Agnes sat bolt upright on her seat in the front row, her ears straining for the slightest sound.

For a few moments the only sounds to be heard were the tinkling of the piano accompanying Sylvia's dance and the gentle thud of Sylvia's feet as she leapt across the stage. Agnes was leaning back in her chair when there was a terrific crash and a sound of thumping from the roof of the theatre. The chandelier that hung above the theatre stalls shook as something pounded on the roof. Agnes screamed and even Sylvia began to look alarmed. Maximilian padded down the rows of seats to spring up on to Agnes's lap.

Outside, the rain hammered down still harder. The sky darkened and there was a rumble of thunder. "You see," said Miss Julier crisply. "It really is just a storm. Now, back to work, Sylvia."

Onstage, Sylvia smoothed the front of her dress and prepared to dance again.

And then Agnes shrieked and pointed up

to the dome of the theatre, her mouth open in horror. All eyes followed to where she was pointing.

On the roof, staring down through the glass dome, was a dark figure in a long flowing dress. Its hair thrashed around wildly in the wind. There was a flash of lightning and the sky lit up, revealing a ghastly, pale face, eyes hollowed and black, the mouth a gash of red, twisted back in a snarl of hate. Agnes screamed again and in a moment the theatre was full of shouts and the thunder of feet as the company ran from the stage. One of the chorus grabbed Sylvia's hand and dragged her towards the wings. Miss Julier motioned desperately for everyone to keep calm. The lightning flashed again and the figure on the roof disappeared from sight.

Maximilian leapt from Agnes's lap and dashed down the aisle, out into the porch. Outside, thunder was rumbling across the sky and the rain was beating down so hard in the twilight that it was difficult to see. Maximilian called out for Oscar, but there was no reply.

He set off for the side of the theatre and clambered up the tendrils of an ivy stem

that snaked up to the roof. The storm had made the stem slippery and the rain beat down into his eyes, blinding him. He was reaching out for a paw-hold in the ivy when the sky was torn apart by a thunderclap so loud it felt like the theatre was shaking, and the scrap of ivy Maximilian clung to tore away from the wall. With a miaow of terror Maximilian clawed at the stem, but with the rain falling full pelt into his eyes it was impossible to find a safe paw-hold. He fell, the blood rushing to his ears. The world went silent for a moment and then Maximilian felt his leg clasped and his paw pushed firmly into a net of intertwined leaves. Maximilian dangled, breathless, from the side of the building and squinted upwards into the night. There was a flash of lightning, illuminating a black cat and one bright-green orb of an eye.

Maximilian gritted his teeth and hauled his way up. He was full of thank-yous, but too breathless to get them out. Oscar patted him on

the shoulder and motioned across the roof. The lightning flashed again, glinting off the glass of the dome. The shadowy figure was nowhere to be seen.

"How long have you been here?" Maximilian gasped. "Did you see who it was?"

Oscar shook his head. "I took the liberty of dashing up when that young lady – Agnes, is it? Well, when she screamed. It must have taken me seconds at most, but…"

He waved a paw once more, taking in the empty roof before them. Maximilian's eyes were adjusting to the gloom. It had been a very peculiar evening, but one thing was clear. There was nobody else on the roof of the theatre.

After dinner the company gathered in the library. The wood-panelled walls, and shelves lined with leather-bound volumes, made the room dark, but in the huge fireplace of polished slate a hearty fire had been lit. The logs crackled

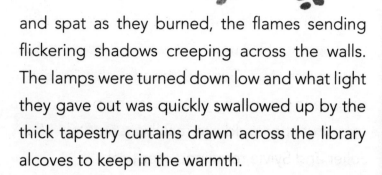

and spat as they burned, the flames sending flickering shadows creeping across the walls. The lamps were turned down low and what light they gave out was quickly swallowed up by the thick tapestry curtains drawn across the library alcoves to keep in the warmth.

Maximilian was curled up on one of the deep-cushioned sofas between Agnes and Sylvia, warming his toes in the heat of the fire and hoping that no one would notice how grubby his paws were. Mrs Garland seemed to have entirely forgotten the issue of the bath, and he wanted to keep it that way. Across from them sat Bunty and Arabella, wrapped up together in one large throw. After what had happened, the company could talk of nothing but the theatre ghost and before Maximilian could say "no one gave me a second helping of salmon tonight", there were ghost stories in the air.

Agnes, once again, told everyone about seeing the Theatre Royal ghost in the costume store. One of the chorus declared he had met the spectre of his uncle late at night coming out of a tavern. Mrs Garland thought she "might" have seen something strange in an opera house once but she could not recall where. Only Miss Julier and Sylvia remained sceptical.

"And now it seems we have woken Lady Celine," said a voice from the corner of the room. A figure uncurled itself from a leather wing chair and Lord Rorston stepped into the light of the fire. Agnes was so startled that she dropped the cushion she had been hiding behind, and Bunty gave a little gasp.

"Papa, I thought you had gone to bed!" she cried.

Lord Rorston motioned towards a square box brimming with rolls of paper and parchments tied up with twine. "Working late, my dear."

Bunty turned to Sylvia and Agnes. "Papa is something of an amateur historian," she explained.

"All our frightful old family papers are in that box," Arabella joined in. "Uncle Maurice is going to turn them into a history of the Fawleys that only the Fawleys will ever read."

She laughed, but Bunty looked dignified. "I'm sure that it will be most interesting once it is finished. Papa is taking great care with it all."

Arabella looked apologetic. "I didn't mean to be rude, Bunts," she said. "I just meant that … well, Uncle Maurice, even you must agree that the mouldy old Fawleys aren't as interesting as the ghostly tales we've been telling this evening."

Lord Rorston smiled at her.

"Fascinating tales," he smiled. "They distracted me from my work. All this talk of ghouls did make me wonder about our family spirit, however. As I said, have we woken the Viscountess?"

Bunty's eyes widened. "Oh, Papa! What if you are right?" She turned to Agnes. "After all, you

70

did see her at the theatre and that's where she is said to appear."

Maximilian thought that if Bunty was trying to frighten Agnes, she was going the right way about it. Agnes's eyes were as big as saucers.

Lord Rorston yawned and stretched. "Well, it's very late and I think I shall retire to bed. Bunty, I think you should be turning in too." He gave a gallant bow to the company, gathered his papers into the box and motioned for Bunty to follow him. Maximilian stared after the two of them, in deep conversation as they headed for the library door, and he felt the tip of his tail tingling. The Rorstons both seemed very eager to make everyone believe in the theatre ghost. He wondered why.

CHAPTER 8
Rattling in the Dark

"Ransacked!" cried Sylvia, throwing her arms up in the air. Agnes stood behind her, her mouth open with shock. It was the next morning and the company had just entered their dressing rooms to find them in a state of complete disarray. Drawers had been pulled out, the contents strewn across the floor. Costumes had been ripped from hangers. One of the locked cabinets had been forced open.

"Who would do this?" Agnes said,

tears springing to her eyes. Then she froze and grabbed at Sylvia's arm. "Oh, Sylvia, you don't think it's *her*, do you?"

Maximilian rolled his eyes. So did Sylvia.

"Not your mouldy old ghost again, Agnes? No, frankly, I don't think it's her."

Agnes sulked. "Well, *who* then?"

Maximilian sniffed the air. There was a strong smell of roses and something tingled in the tip of his tail. One thing he was sure of, ghosts did not use perfume. Whoever had turned the theatre over had been very human. But why? After his recent adventure foiling a daring jewel thief his mind went instantly to theft, but what could be worth stealing in an old theatre? Surely a competent thief would head for the castle itself, which was bound to be stuffed full of Arabella's jewels. It was very curious.

The company set to tidying up, a task that was made more than usually trying for Sylvia by

Agnes insisting on stopping every five minutes to declare that she was sure she had "heard something" or "felt a ghostly presence". Eventually they had everything tidy again, and after lunch (pilchard sandwiches, which Sylvia was very generous with) Maximilian went to join Oscar, and the two of them spent the rest of the day "voling" in the woods behind the rose garden. Oscar caught three and Maximilian only one, but since Maximilian knew that he would be able to sneak a little salmon at supper that evening, this was considered fair. When the clock on the West Tower of the castle struck seven o'clock, Maximilian made his way back to the theatre to collect Sylvia and Agnes. The company were packing up to make their way over to dress for dinner but Sylvia was standing in the middle of the stage, her mouth pulled into a pout.

"We're almost perfect," she wheedled. "Can't we run though just one more time?"

Miss Julier glanced at her wristwatch. "If you promise to lock up carefully, Sylvia, you can stay, but I expect you to be in the dining hall when the gong goes. You'll have to be extra quick changing."

Agnes watched longingly as the rest of the company left the theatre, the men of the chorus doing elaborate tumbles across Lord Fawley's long front lawn. Under the watchful eye of Maximilian, they ran through the scene one more time, with Maximilian helping them out by miaowing "a little higher" and "you are not quite in time" and "can I have a snack now?"

Agnes was halfway through the most difficult part of her solo when there was a sudden rattling. Agnes froze, her mouth still open to soar up to the note that made people clutch their hearts and murmur "wonderful".

"What was that?" she whispered.

The theatre was silent for a few seconds, then the rattling began again, louder and more urgent. Sylvia moved close to Agnes and the two of them glanced around nervously. Maximilian sprang to his feet and peered into the wings.

"It's nothing," Sylvia said. "Just the wind, I suppose."

Agnes grabbed at Sylvia's hand. "It doesn't sound much like the wind," she whimpered. She glanced quickly up at the dome of the roof.

The rattling stopped as suddenly as it had begun. Sylvia breathed a sigh of relief and looked at Maximilian.

"See, old puss," she said with a smile. "Nothing to worry about after all."

And then they were plunged into darkness.

Agnes screamed.

"It must be the electrics," Sylvia cried.

Maximilian jumped on to the stage, trying to find Agnes and Sylvia in the pitch black. He brushed against one of their feet, hoping that it would be comforting, but Agnes just screamed even louder.

All at once the lights came back on. Agnes had her hands over her face and was still shrieking.

Sylvia looked wildly around the theatre. "Over there!" she cried, pointing at the wide oak doors that led out into the lobby.

A tall figure dressed in a flowing midnight-blue gown was disappearing through them, a figure with dark flowing curls and stars on her dress.

"It's her!" Agnes shrieked. "It's the Viscountess!"

Maximilian growled. He leapt from the stage and fled down through the rows of seats and through the doors out into the night. The moon was hidden behind the clouds, making the shapes of the garden loom up at him from out of the dark. The statues and hedges seemed larger than they had in the day. Ahead of him the house glowed with light. He glanced from side to side. One of the statues shivered and set off across the lawn. It was the figure from the theatre. Maximilian set off after it, gaining on it quickly as it hurried towards the side of the house.

It's huffing quite loudly for a ghost, Maximilian thought. *It sounds very out of breath.*

As the figure reached the corner of the house, Maximilian caught hold of the edge of its skirt between his teeth and pulled. The figure whirled round.

"Get off that!" said a voice, and the figure

pulled roughly at the fabric. There was a ripping sound as the dress tore and Maximilian tumbled back into the grass, a scrap of blue fabric caught in his mouth.

He watched the figure disappear round the side of the house. His head was reeling. Surely ghosts could not speak. Maximilian's tail twitched. This was no ghost!

CHAPTER 9
An Unexpected Guest

Agnes flung open the door of the castle. Maximilian bounded in after her, the shred of velvet safely clamped in his mouth.

"Stop being so silly," Sylvia said firmly. "There's no such thing as ghosts. It was probably one of the footmen playing a prank on us."

"It was *her*," Agnes wailed, flinging out a hand towards the portrait of Celine at the top of the stairs.

Maximilian patted Agnes's ankle with

his paw. If she would only take a look at the scrap of fabric she would realise that whoever wore it had been very human. Agnes ignored him and continued to sob.

"What on earth is the matter, my dears?" Lord Fawley cried, coming out of the library with Arabella and Lord Rorston. He crossed the hall quickly, a look of great concern on his face. As he reached them, Bunty came dashing down the stairs, her hair in disarray and her face very pink.

"She thinks she saw a ghost," Sylvia explained, patting Agnes on the arm. "I've been trying to convince her that it's probably just someone playing a joke."

"Probably a result of too many ghoulish stories late at night," sighed Lord Fawley. "I think we've had quite enough of this haunted portrait nonsense. My dears, you must have been hard at work. You've not had time to dress."

"Never mind," said Arabella, who was looking delightful in a fringed teal dress with little rosebuds on the shoulders. "It's a silly tradition anyway, and what you have on is charming."

Maximilian saw Bunty's mouth twitch a little at this. She was dressed less smartly than Arabella in a rather drab-coloured dress with a lace edging. Maximilian felt a little sorry for her. It was rather mortifying not to look one's best when one was in company.

Bunty dropped down to tickle Maximilian on the nose. "Hello, lovely puss," she whispered. "Aren't you handsome."

Maximilian looked up into her smiling face and felt himself melting. She was so awfully sweet. Agnes was being very silly at the moment. Sylvia could think of nothing but perfecting her dances, and Mrs Garland and Miss Julier were both too caught up in trying to get the show together to pay him much attention. It was not very loyal to admit it but Bunty was the only human who was being particularly nice to him.

"What's this, puss?" Bunty asked, taking hold

of the scrap of fabric. Maximilian gritted his teeth but Bunty pulled determinedly. "Nasty stuff for a puss to have," she said, barely glancing at the scrap before folding it into her palm, out of sight. Then she smiled and tickled him under the chin again before standing up and taking Arabella's arm.

Maximilian gave out a plaintive miaow of "that could be valuable evidence" but, as usual, no one was listening.

Lord Fawley was about to lead them all into dinner when the door of the castle was flung open and a pinched-looking little man with a pointed beard stood in the doorway.

"Maurice! I come. You call for me and I come!" The man executed a most unnecessarily complex series of bows.

Lord Rorston threw out his arms to welcome the intruder. "Antonio! Fawley, this is my very good friend Antonio, one of the most celebrated psychical researchers in all of London."

The little man carried out another round of ridiculous bows and bounded forwards to Lord Fawley, who was looking rather confused.

"Lord Rorston was kind enough to say that I could accompany him on this most interesting visit," he said.

Maximilian's ears pricked up and he felt the end of his tail tingle. The man called Antonio had a very familiar voice. Maximilian was sure that he had heard it before, and quite recently too. He craned his head round Agnes's ankle to get a proper look at him,

"Antonio is fascinated by your haunted portrait, Robert," said Lord Rorston. "I took the liberty of inviting him to join us for a few days. You don't mind, do you?"

Maximilian thought that Lord Fawley looked as though he minded very much, but he was far too much of a gentleman to say so. It was most peculiar of Lord Rorston to invite a stranger to Lord Fawley's house, and for a family party too.

The man called Antonio bowed again. "I have brought some equipment with me, Your Lordship. Sensitive equipment. Scientific equipment. It will detect your ghost and perhaps we can make contact with it. But I insist that no one else but me has access to it. You understand? No prying by maids and footmen. I will not allow it!"

Lord Fawley looked a little put out at being ordered around in his own house.

"It's his way," Lord Rorston explained. "He is very particular. But he's the talk of London, I assure you."

Maximilian frowned at this. He had never heard of Antonio, and he was a very well-informed cat. The great front door of the castle swung open again and Lord Fawley's footmen entered, staggering under the weight of a number of large crates.

Antonio went into instant flurries of concern. "Careful! Careful!" he cried.

Lord Fawley rolled his eyes and beckoned one of the footmen over to him. He murmured something in the man's ear and with a brisk nod and a click of the heels the footman strode off towards the staircase, followed by the crate-carriers. Antonio accompanied them, fussing about needing a room with a nice view.

"It is most important," he insisted to the footman in charge. "I fade without a view of nature."

Maximilian stared at him. What a fusspot! He was sure now that he recognised the man's voice. And there was something else as well. Every sentence was punctuated with a strange twisting gesture of his right hand, the fingers pointing upwards to the ceiling. Maximilian wracked his brain. Where *had* he seen that before?

"You get used to him," Lord Rorston said once the little man was out of sight. "He will amuse Arabella. A psychical researcher at her party.

None of her friends can claim to have someone catch a ghost for their birthday present!"

Catch a ghost? thought Maximilian. *I nearly caught a "ghost" earlier myself. I wonder who it really was.* If only Bunty hadn't taken away his only shred of evidence, but then humans were always getting in the way.

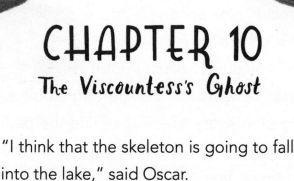

CHAPTER 10
The Viscountess's Ghost

"I think that the skeleton is going to fall into the lake," said Oscar.

It was the next morning and the two friends were watching a team of men in overalls putting the finishing touches to a ghostly galleon, hung with cobwebs, that had been winched on to Lord Fawley's ornamental lake an hour earlier. Just after dawn, two large trucks emblazoned with "Cooper's Theatrical Equipment Co." had drawn up to the gates of the castle and a small army of workers had descended to create the perfect atmosphere for Arabella's Halloween masked ball. Hundreds of pumpkin-shaped lanterns had been brought out to hang from every tree and to line the paths around the gardens. Witches' broomsticks were hung from wires that trailed from tree to tree and up to the towers of the castle itself. At the flick of a switch the brooms would fly down the wires over the heads of Lord Fawley's guests.

On the galleon, two men were involved in a tug-of-war over where the skeleton hanging from the rigging would look best. Oscar raised an eyebrow at Maximilian and, as if on cue, the skeleton fell from the ship into the lake, followed by one of the men.

It was all very interesting to watch, but Maximilian's

89

tummy was beginning to rumble a little. He eyed the fish in the lake very keenly but decided that it was probably bad manners to poach from your host's lake. "I hear that they have started to make the salmon mousse in the kitchen," he said.

Oscar grinned and they set off towards the castle to see if the cook was in a good mood.

As they rounded the corner of one of Lord Fawley's magnificent yew hedges, they saw Bunty sitting on her own on a bench by the rose garden. She was engrossed in a satin-covered book, deep frown lines running across her brow as she pored over the pages. Arabella, dressed in a crisp tweed skirt and cashmere jumper, was crossing the lawn towards her, but Bunty was too taken up with her book to notice her friend. It was not till Arabella dropped herself on to the bench beside her that Bunty realised she was there at all.

"Arabella, you frightened the life out of me!" she cried, dropping the book. Folded pieces

of paper spilled out from between its pages and Bunty scrabbled to collect them. Arabella leaned over and picked one up.

"What on earth is all this, Bunts? It looks like letters," she said, turning the paper over in her hands. Bunty snatched it away and blushed as she tucked the folded paper back into the book.

"It's ... nothing. Let's talk about the party."

Arabella pouted. "Well, this sounds very mysterious. Oh, Bunty, it's not love letters, is it? Who? You have to tell your dearest friend!"

Bunty slipped the book into one of the roomy pockets of her cardigan and shook her head. "I can't tell anyone yet. Not even you."

Arabella sighed. "Why not? Oh, it is love letters, isn't it! Is it awfully romantic? But why must it be a secret? Is he something awfully low, like a farmer? Will your father be utterly furious? Oh, Bunts, how lovely. But you're right, we'll talk no more about it. Come and see the galleon. It's looking wonderful and there's going to be fireworks over it at midnight as we all take our masks off!"

Maximilian watched them walk across the lawn. Was Bunty hiding a love affair from her father? Maximilian was, at heart, wonderfully romantic. His favourite shows at the Theatre Royal always involved doomed lovers torn apart by cruel parents. He instantly cast Bunty in the role of the tragic maiden, separated from her dearest love. Perhaps, once he had solved the mystery of the theatre hauntings and the curious ransacking of the dressing rooms, he could help the star-crossed lovers…

Oscar gave a little cough. "I believe someone mentioned salmon mousse?" he said.

Lord Fawley's cook turned out to be very generous when it came to portions, and after licking the last morsels of salmon from his paws and cleaning up his tail, which had somehow trailed in his dish, Maximilian was ready for one of his eight daily catnaps. As he was settling his head on his paws in the library, however, he heard Lord Rorston and the man called Antonio pass the door, deep in conversation. Maximilian sighed. He was so tired, but he could feel that familiar tingling in his tail. There was something very odd about Antonio's presence at Fawley Castle and he was not sure that he believed the man's story about "catching a ghost". So he slipped from his chair and crept out into the hallway. He was just in time to see the two men mount the stairs, heading to the landing where the painting was. Being careful not to get too close, Maximilian followed them.

"... planning this for months," Lord Rorston was saying. "Having the theatre folk here has been a little awkward but they shouldn't cause us too much trouble."

Antonio did not say anything. He took a silver box out of his waistcoat pocket and turned it over in his fingers. He pressed a button on the side and a tape measure spooled down across the floor.

"Precision is *everything*," he murmured, stretching the tape measure from the wall where Lady Celine's portrait hung to the top of the stairs. "Oh, hello, small cat," he said, noticing Maximilian. Antonio tipped his head to one side and stared at Maximilian keenly. "A handsome fellow," he remarked. "I would like to work with cats. They are very jolly. Do you think he can be trained?"

Maximilian let out his "how dare you suggest such a thing!" miaow. Trained? The very thought of it! Dogs could be trained, of course, but, as everyone knew, they were even less intelligent than humans.

"Stick to the plan," Lord Rorston said firmly. "As we agreed. At midnight she appears, Arabella gets the fright of her life and then leave the rest to me." He looked up at the portrait and laughed. "Trained cats, indeed! Everyone knows you can't train a cat. They're not as clever as dogs."

Maximilian had heard enough.

He was still smarting over Lord Rorston's rudeness late that night, curled up on Sylvia's bed and musing on everything he had heard. Why on earth was the man planning to scare Arabella on her birthday? What did he mean by "leave the rest to me"? Maximilian added these mysteries to the ones he already had – who had been ransacking the theatre, and who was dressing up as the Viscountess. But there were too many pieces of this particular puzzle and, try as he might, he could not make them fit together. There was only one thing to do. Maximilian set to giving his tail a groom.

He had just got it looking utterly perfect, and was feeling much more clever as a result, when Agnes and Sylvia fell through the door, giggling and with bundles of fabric, lace trimmings and beads spilling from their arms. Sylvia dropped her pile on the bed, squashing Maximilian's tail. He let out an exasperated sigh and whisked it under his paws.

"Just look what we found in the theatre, Max!" Agnes said, shaking out a bright-orange organza gown with a handkerchief hem. The light evening breeze from the window made the hem flutter, and as the moonlight caught the silvery braid in the fabric it shimmered like flames.

"Isn't it just perfect!" Agnes cried, holding the dress to herself and whirling round. "We rescued some old jewellery from a tea chest too, so I'm going to sew the sparkliest bits on to this and go as fire for the costume ball tomorrow night."

Maximilian reached out a paw to the pile of gems that Sylvia had dropped on to the bed. It was a mass of chains and beads and twisted metal.

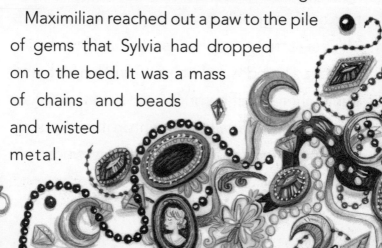

Chunks of glass cut to look like precious gemstones hung from some of the chains, their brilliance dulled by layers of dust.

"Some of these do look awfully pretty, you know, Sylvia," Agnes said, picking up a crescent-shaped piece and blowing the dust off it. Maximilian coughed as the dust went up his nose, and he tucked his tail more firmly under his paws to stop it from being utterly ruined. Agnes gave the piece a polish on the edge of her sleeve and held it up to the light.

"It looks like a tiny moon," she sighed. "Isn't it lovely. There are lots of them – ouch!"

Agnes held up a finger on which a tiny bubble of blood was pooling.

"The setting must be broken," Sylvia said. "Give it a good wash. I hate to think how many germs there must be on it."

Agnes dashed to the basin on the dressing table and sloshed a good deal of water into it from a nearby jug. Maximilian patted at the bits of jewellery that were scattered across Agnes's bed. There were lots of moon shapes, but then there were moons everywhere in the castle. Each of the window panes had crescent moons delicately etched into the corners. There were moons carved into the top of each bed and delicate curves of crescents danced around each of the lamps. He tucked a claw round one of the sparkling moon-shaped gems that was snagged on a delicate filigree pendant and tugged. With one pull it worked free and clattered to the floor.

"Clever old Max," Sylvia said. "You can untangle them for us while we get on with the sewing. The ball is tomorrow night and we both need gorgeous costumes and masks."

For the next few hours, Agnes and Sylvia sat curled up on their beds sewing jewels on to their dresses. Maximilian had disentangled all the moons from the chains and ribbons that were twisted round them and Sylvia arranged them

prettily at the shoulder of her ice-blue gown. She was going as a flash of moonlight to honour Lady Celine, and the moons were set into a swirl of sparkling crescents on a frill that cascaded from one shoulder down to the neckline of her silver dress, ending in a huge full moon-shaped crystal.

As the clock neared midnight, there was a knocking at the door.

Agnes swung herself off the bed and opened it. The corridor outside was completely empty.

"That's odd," she said, shutting it again. "I must be hearing things."

The door had barely closed when the knocking began again, louder this time. Agnes yanked it open but there was no one there.

At the end of the corridor there was a flicker of candlelight. Maximilian's tail twitched and he slipped past Agnes out into the corridor. The candlelight flickered again and moved away, towards the stairs.

Maximilian followed the candlelight through the house. At the last turn of the stairs he came to the gallery above the Great Hall. At the end of the gallery a lantern hung in mid-air. From the shadows a figure emerged, a woman in a long blue gown. Her face was a mask of white with hollowed pits of dark where her eyes should be. She put a finger to her lips and then pointed towards the portrait, her mouth opening in a silent, horrible scream.

Maximilian felt his fur stand on end. He heard a shriek behind him and he realised that Sylvia must have followed him. The lantern flickered, illuminating the terrible face still more brightly, then in an instant it was extinguished and the woman in the blue dress vanished.

Maximilian darted down the corridor. As he did so he could hear, once more, the footsteps he had heard on the first night. They seemed to be coming towards him, but, squinting hard into the shadows at the end of the corridor, he could see no one ahead. The footsteps grew closer. They were almost on top of him, then they started to fade away. Maximilian felt a chill run through him and he was aware that his paws were shaking. He took several deep breaths, his eyes darting round. The moon broke through the clouds outside, illuminating some of the portraits hanging round the hall. Eyes loomed out of the dark paintwork. The teeth of a horse leered at him out of a painting at the end of the hall. Maximilian shuddered. How he wished that Oscar were here, being sensible and telling him stories that did *not* involve ghosts and creeping things in the night.

"Puss, let's get out of here," Sylvia whispered, her voice breaking a little. Maximilian turned to go back to her, when suddenly Sylvia let out an ear-splitting scream that echoed off the walls and marble floors of the castle. She lifted a shaking hand and pointed towards the end of the hall.

"Look!"

Maximilian looked where Sylvia was pointing, to the great portrait of Lady Celine that hung over the hall. The moonlight lit up the gilding on the frame, picking out the crescent moons etched into its woodwork. But Lady Celine's face did not shine out of the dark paintwork as the other portraits had done. The frame was empty except for the dappled blue and grey background of the painting.

Lady Celine had disappeared from her own portrait.

Sylvia's screams soon woke the house. Maids and footmen came running from the narrow staircases that led to the upper floors. Mrs Garland came dashing down the stairs behind Sylvia, wrapped in a dressing gown and with a poker in her hand. From the other side of the gallery Lord Fawley pushed his way past gawping housemaids and demanded to know what was going on.

Sylvia was tearfully trying to explain when there was another scream, this

time from Arabella, who had just arrived on the gallery and seen the portrait. All colour drained from her face and she fainted into the arms of a convenient footman. The gallery exploded with noise. One of the younger footmen burst into tears; a housemaid began to loudly tell the story of Lady Celine to a group of wide-eyed kitchen maids. It seemed that everyone had a tale to tell about how they "once saw her drifting across the lawns, though of course it might have been a badger". In the midst of all the fuss the butler huffed down the staircase and rattled the dinner gong until there was silence.

"Thank you, Briggs," said Lord Fawley. He looked round the assembled company, looking far from his usual genial self. "I don't know what has happened this evening, or who is behind this tomfoolery, but I tell you all this. There is no such thing as ghosts. This is all just a foolish and rather cruel prank. However, that portrait is a valuable artwork and a piece of considerable sentimental value to the family. I do not wish to ruin Arabella's birthday so I will give whoever is responsible until her party to return it before I ring the police. Now, go to bed, all of you!"

His face softened as he turned to Arabella, who was reviving a little, and motioned for footmen to carry the girl back to her room.

"Back to bed, you two," said Mrs Garland, putting a hand on Sylvia's arm and leading her and Agnes towards their room. Maximilian hung back, his mind racing. It had been only this morning that he had heard Lord Rorston and Antonio talking about something to scare everyone at midnight. Was this it? He wracked his brain but could not remember seeing Lord Rorston appear with everyone after Sylvia's screams. The man could have played the part of the Viscountess. But how had he made the portrait disappear?

Maximilian decided to investigate. He took a flying leap on to the sideboard that stood underneath the portrait. Balancing very carefully on his back toes, he was able to reach up to the frame and take a closer look at it.

It was very poorly executed, the paint slapped on in great daubs. It looked as though it had been painted very hastily indeed and there was frayed canvas peeping out from the edge of the frame. Maximilian reached out a paw and patted the painting, and when he drew his paw away it was smeared with oil paint, the dark grey of the background staining his beautiful fur.

This isn't the portrait at all! thought Maximilian. *Someone has cut the painting out of the frame and replaced it with this mess. It must have been done after everyone went to sleep, and whoever did it has stolen the real painting.*

Maximilian looked around the empty hall. If someone had dressed up as the Viscountess, then they must have been hiding somewhere while everyone was dashing around the gallery. He leapt to the floor and padded over to the corner where he had last seen the figure. There were drops of candle wax on the floor. Maximilian patted one with his paw. It was cool, but still soft, and the pads of his paw left little prints on the droplet.

He peered around. Lord Fawley's maids were *most* particular about dusting, which was wonderful for those cats who were fastidious about their tails, but unfortunately meant that there were no useful footprints for him to follow. He nosed around in the corner and peeked behind one of the tapestries that hung from the wall, but there were no clues there either.

Maximilian turned his attention to the beautiful wood panelling that lined the walls of the gallery. It was polished to perfection, the glossy surface gleaming in the moonlight. An intricately carved border with Lord Fawley's family crest of ivy leaves and crescent moons ran round the ceiling and floor. Maximilian lifted himself up on to his hind legs and closely inspected the join between two panels, hoping that there might be a secret door to be found, but after picking away at the join with one of his claws he gave a little miaow of defeat.

He was pondering where to investigate next when his eye caught something on one of the panels. The crescent moons on the crests along the border all faced to the left, but one moon, in the middle of one of the panels, faced to the right. Maximilian's tail began to tingle and he pressed his face up to the crest to examine it more closely. Was he mistaken, or was the wood a little more clearly etched out, almost as if the moon was a button? With a paw that trembled a little, Maximilian reached out and pressed the crescent moon. There was a faint click and the panel swung open a few centimetres. Maximilian pulled the panel towards him and squinted into the dark.

He had found the ghost's hiding place.

CHAPTER 12
The Ghost's Walk

It was a narrow space, just wide enough for one human to squeeze through, and was riddled with cobwebs and dust that made Maximilian shudder. There was no light except for tiny shafts that filtered through from cracks in the panelling. As Maximilian crept down the passage he could feel his paws becoming smothered with grimy dust. His beautiful tail grew heavy with cobwebs and his ears prickled with spiders tickling behind them as he dislodged their homes.

He pressed on, trying to ignore how disgusting his fur felt. It was almost impossible to see at all, but he strained his eyes looking for clues and swept the floor with his paws, in case the ghost had dropped anything. After a few minutes one of his claws snagged on something and Maximilian stumbled around in the dark, trying to snatch hold of it. It was a small piece of cloth. Shuddering at how dirty it must be, Maximilian picked it up with his teeth and grimaced at the taste of dust.

He was so engrossed in resisting the urge to spit it out, and trying *not* to think about whether he had just swallowed a spider, that he missed his footing and was sent tumbling downwards. The passageway had opened on to a set of stone steps and as Maximilian bounced down them he let out a miaow of alarm. His claws scrabbled against the stonework, but he kept falling till he landed with a bump on a flagstone floor and the scrap of cloth floated down to land on his nose.

Maximilian put out a paw to feel for his

surroundings. The narrow walls were still on either side and, to his alarm, there was stone in front of him too. He steeled himself not to panic and sniffed the air. A breath of fresh, cold air coursed over his face and gave him hope that somewhere there was a way out. He placed his shoulder against the cool stone in front of him and felt his way along it, pushing gently. There was the click of a latch and a creak as the stone swung away from him, and Maximilian bounded out into the night air, taking down great gulps of it to try to rid himself of the taste of the dust and cobwebs. Behind

112

him, the stone door swung shut again, sealing itself neatly into the walls of the castle.

Maximilian looked around. He was outside the castle, near the rose gardens. The ornamental hedges loomed above him, great shadows in the night, but there was no sign of the ghostly figure from the gallery. The night hung around him, silent and still, and the feel of the soft grass beneath his paws was a welcome change from the dirty floor of the passageway.

He dropped the scrap of cloth to the floor and spread it out. It was a square piece of fine silk, carefully edged with dark thread. In one corner was a crest with a leaping pike and a sycamore leaf. *It's a handkerchief*, thought Maximilian. *But this is not Lord Fawley's crest*. He peered at something stitched on the edge of the cloth.

In the corner of the handkerchief was an embroidered monogram in florid script. It was the letter "R".

"So it is Lord Rorston!" Oscar said.

It was the next day and they were sitting by the ornamental lake, watching as the final touches were made to the decorations for Arabella's Halloween party that evening. Every pathway was lined with pumpkin lanterns and the ornamental gardens had black cat statues set to look as though they were strolling through the flowerbeds or leaping from the trees. In the middle of the garden a huge topiary cat had been cut from the middle of the yew hedge.

Maximilian nodded. "Yes! He must have painted over the portrait, then dressed up as the Viscountess and knocked on Agnes and Sylvia's door to make sure that someone saw him. Then he slipped away down the passageway while everyone was fussing around in the gallery."

"But why?" asked Oscar. "Why go to all this trouble?"

Maximilian thought about this.

"That is what I can't work out," he said. "We know that Lord Rorston has plans to scare everyone, and that he and Antonio were measuring something in the upstairs gallery. And now we know that Lord Rorston has been dressing up as the Viscountess."

Something twitched at the back of his mind, a memory of Agnes staring at Lady Celine's portrait in horror, of Bunty telling them what would cause the Viscountess to start her hauntings. Maximilian gasped as it fell into place!

"The legend says that the Viscountess will

only start to haunt the castle when the theatre is opened!" he cried. "Lord Rorston must be pretending to be her to make us think that she is angry with us for opening it! But why?"

"It sounds almost as though he wants to keep you all away from the building," Oscar said.

Maximilian thought of the ransacked dressing rooms and the appearance of that ghastly face on the roof of the theatre. Had these been staged to frighten the company?

"That must be it!" he said. "What if he *wants* us to believe in the theatre ghost, so that the company stop working in the theatre? What if it was him who ransacked the dressing rooms? He must have been looking for something in there. Something he doesn't want anyone to find before he does!"

Oscar nodded appreciatively. "It all fits. Do we search the theatre?"

Maximilian shook his head. "First we search Lord Rorston's room!"

CHAPTER 13
A Secret Uncovered

A few minutes later Oscar and Maximilian were creeping along the corridor towards Lord Rorston's room on the second floor of the castle. The maids were busy making the rooms ready for the party guests arriving that afternoon, and there was bustle and hurry everywhere. Every bedroom on the second floor was wide open and in the middle of the corridor stood a gleaming trolley full of pressed and starched linen and antique coverlets all ready to be whisked on to beds full of

plumped-up pillows.

Maximilian peeked in at each door, looking for a sign that it was Lord Rorston's room. As they were rounding the corner at the end of one corridor they spotted the man himself in discussion with Bunty. Her head was hanging low and she looked most upset.

"There's no use in sulking," Lord Rorston was saying, his face firm. "Hand it over and we'll say no more about it."

Bunty shifted her feet and dug a hand into her cardigan pocket, drawing out the book that Maximilian and Oscar had seen her reading the day before. She hid it behind her back, her thumb holding it open at one page, and looked up at her father pleadingly.

"Please can I keep it just a little longer?" she said, but Lord Rorston shook his head.

"These are private papers, Bunty. I should never have let you read it in the first place. Now, hand it over, please."

Behind her back, Bunty carefully tore a page out of the book and crumpled it up into her hand, then handed the book over to her father.

"Good girl," he muttered. "Now, off to Arabella with you. She'll be wanting help with some nonsensical costume."

Lord Rorston opened the door of the room behind him while Bunty strode off down the corridor. As she passed Maximilian and Oscar she moved to slip the crumpled paper into her pocket, but it missed and fell to the floor. Bunty went on her way without noticing.

Maximilian snatched up the paper and sped off after her, weaving round her ankles, but she merely nudged him aside with her foot.

"Not now, cat. Find someone else to bother." And she was gone.

"So what now?" Oscar asked as Maximilian rejoined him.

"I suppose we wait," Maximilian said, and

wait they did. They waited till the lunch bell went, when Lord Rorston left his room and Maximilian's tummy had begun to rumble. Then they waited for a further half-hour till one of the maids threw the door open to change the bedding. They slipped in behind her and hid under the bed until the coast was clear.

"Your stomach will give us away one of these days," Oscar said as they crept out from their hiding place. Maximilian pouted and pulled his tummy in. It gave another loud roar of complaint. Breakfast seemed a long time ago.

Lord Rorston's room was very tidy, and indeed a little sparse for a lord. His dressing table held only a hairbrush, a small pot of pomade and a curling iron for his moustaches. A single briefcase sat on a writing desk. Maximilian leapt on to the chair and pushed at the clasp. He half expected it to be locked, but it sprang open and a pile of papers spilled out and fluttered to the floor.

"They must be some of the papers that he has

been looking at for Lord Fawley," Maximilian said. "The ones he was reading in the library that night when everyone was telling ghost stories."

He squinted at the pages more closely. They were full of diagrams that felt very familiar. They looked a little like the plans of the Theatre Royal that Monsieur Lavroche had on the wall in his office. There were stalls and boxes carefully drawn in black ink as rows of tiny chairs. The stage formed a curve across the page, with the plan of the dressing rooms and fly gallery sketched out to the side.

"These are theatre plans!" he said. "They must be of Lord Fawley's theatre."

"More proof that Lord Rorston is looking for something in there?" suggested Oscar.

"That's not all," said Maximilian, pointing a paw at a square drawn in the middle of one of the plans. "I've seen this before. There are plans of the Theatre Royal in Monsieur Lavroche's office and there is a symbol like this in the middle of the stage where the trapdoor is."

Oscar peered at the paper. "But this looks as though it is on the roof," he said.

Maximilian nodded. "Do you remember that night of the storm?" he asked. "How we couldn't work out how the Viscountess disappeared from the theatre roof? There must be a trapdoor."

"An escape route. How ingenious," murmured Oscar.

Pleased to have solved one mystery, Maximilian nudged the plans aside and rifled through the other papers. What a nuisance it was to not be able to read. There were more loose papers and some very old pictures, and at the bottom of the case was Bunty's book. Maximilian pulled it out with his paw and tried to nudge it on to the desk, but it slipped from his grasp and clattered to the floor, the clasp springing open and loose leaves spilling out.

"Bunty's letters!" Maximilian cried, jumping down to try to put the damage right, but Oscar reached out a paw and stopped him.

"Those aren't letters," he said, and something in his voice made Maximilian pause. "And I would bet my best vole-catching night on it that these were not written by Bunty," Oscar continued. "This is a diary, and just look at the date! Eighteen twenty-six."

"How on earth did you know that?" Maximilian said. He eyed Oscar carefully. "Oscar, can you read? Like the humans do?"

Oscar nodded. "Of course. It's a very necessary skill."

"Where did you—" Maximilian stopped himself. Oscar loved to tell stories. He had stories about how he lost his eye (this week's account involved a daring rescue at sea and an unfortunate encounter with a swordfish), and stories about incredible adventures on the rooftops of London. But Oscar never told stories about his past, about what his life had been like before he met Maximilian. And Maximilian did not like to pry. Instead, he stared at the diary.

"It's written in a beautiful hand," murmured Oscar, and then he started to read.

"Roger is talking of a new building project in the grounds. It sounds frivolous but I suppose I must support him. He has invited an architect down to the estate for the weekend…"

Oscar broke off. "It must be talking about the theatre. I wonder whose diary it is." He pulled the pages back, trying not to damage them. There were loose leaves from where Bunty had broken the binding tearing out the paper that

Maximilian had picked up. On the front page of the diary, written in the same beautiful slanted hand, was a single word. Oscar read it out.

"*Celine.*"

Maximilian gasped. "Lady Celine's diary!" he said.

Oscar looked around the room. "Where did you put the other page?" he asked.

Maximilian leapt up on to the dressing table and nudged the crumpled-up paper to the floor, where Oscar smoothed it out and began to read.

"*... Roger runs through our money like water and now he says that my jewels must be sold to pay for more costumes. Nothing in this house is safe. My gold bangles have gone from my case and the silver goblets have disappeared from the dining room. I cannot bear that my precious Moonrise should be sold for such silliness. The stones are too valuable to me. I shall break up the tiara this evening and hide my beautiful*" *stones in the one place he will never think of raiding – his ridiculous theatre. I will go at night by candlelight. I will use the passageway behind the upper gallery and be back before he notices I am gone."*

Oscar paused. "What is this Moonrise?" he asked.

"It's the tiara on the Viscountess's portrait," said Maximilian. "It was lost to the family. Arabella should have received it on her eighteenth birthday but no one knows what became of it."

"Until now," Oscar said, smiling. "It must be in the theatre. That must be what Lord Rorston has been looking for. Well, that explains why he wanted to keep everyone away from the place."

Maximilian frowned. Something didn't fit.

"But Lord Rorston didn't have this information," he said slowly. "Bunty had it. And Bunty tried to hide it from him."

"Bunty?" said Oscar.

Maximilian did not respond. His mind was working over all the clues that they had of Lord Rorston's guilt. One in particular stood out. Had he made a mistake?

"That handkerchief could belong to her," he mused. "The 'R' and the Rorston crest. It could just as well be Bunty's, not Lord Rorston's."

Maximilian's mind was still working, and it was coming to rather unpleasant conclusions. It did not seem like the act of a gentleman to accuse a lady, particularly one as sweet as Bunty. Could Bunty really have climbed on to the roof of the theatre to impersonate Lady Celine and ripped the painting out of its frame? There was only one way to find out, but it made him shudder to think of how many rules of etiquette he was about to break.

"Oscar," he said. "We will have to search the lady's room."

Oscar nodded. He grasped the piece of diary

in his teeth. "In case we need to explain matters to the humans," he explained.

Not for the first time, Maximilian wished that cats could talk.

CHAPTER 14
A Breach of Etiquette

Getting into Bunty's room proved easier than getting into Lord Rorston's but Maximilian felt himself blushing under his fur as he slipped past one of the maids, who was changing the water in a vase of peonies by a window seat.

Outside, the sound of workmen had been swapped for the purr of car motors as Lord Fawley's guests arrived for afternoon tea. Maximilian sprang on to the windowsill to see a long parade of the most exquisite cars in cream, powder

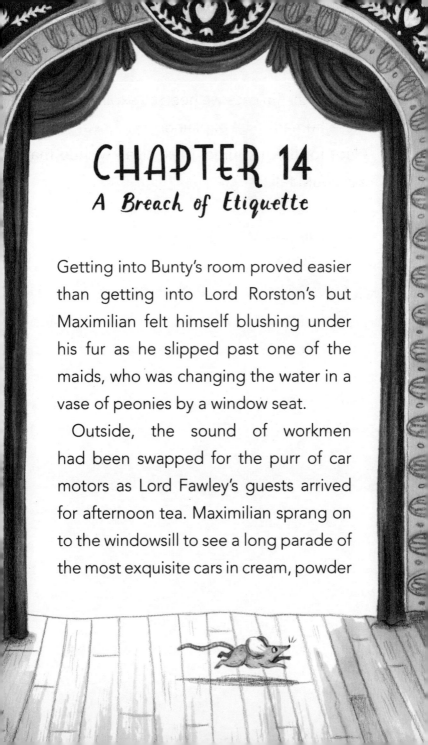

blue and ivy green make its way down the gravel drive to the front of the castle. There were cries of recognition and laughter as friends greeted one another, and Lord Fawley dashed from one group to another, ushering them all towards the castle ballroom where a tea had been laid on for their arrival. Arabella was nowhere to be seen, but Maximilian could see Bunty talking to a lady in a broad-brimmed hat tied on with a flowing sunflower-print scarf. With any luck she would be too distracted to come back upstairs and interrupt their search. He turned back to look around the room. Bunty's luggage was piled neatly in the corner, a smart set of matching blue cases with leather piping.

Oscar padded over to them and tried the catches, but they were all locked. He glanced at Maximilian and winked with his one good eye. Then he flicked out a claw, placed it in the keyhole of the top case and leaned his ear next to the lock. A wiggle of his paw and the lock sprang open.

Maximilian gasped. "Where did you learn—"

"Best not to know," said Oscar, grinning. "A story for another day." He nudged open the case and leaned over to look inside. "Well I never…"

In the corner of the case was a rolled-up piece of canvas. With a heavy heart, Maximilian pulled it out and slipped his claw under the narrow piece of twine that bound it. The canvas sprang open and unfurled across the floor, revealing a dark-blue gown, a tiara of sparkling diamonds and the beautiful face of Lady Celine.

Bunty had the missing portrait.

Maximilian stared at the painting miserably. He had thought that when he caught who was responsible for all the peculiar goings-on he would be proud and happy, as he had been when he had solved his last case, at the Theatre Royal. But now that Bunty might be involved he just felt confused. He rather liked Bunty and she had been very kind to him.

"But at dinner that first night, Bunty was in the dining room, so she couldn't have been the one making the ghostly footsteps in the gallery..." Maximilian's voice fell away as he remembered that Bunty had left the room before him. She had gone to bed with a headache.

"What did the Viscountess say about the passageway in her diary?" he asked Oscar, half dreading the answer.

Oscar smoothed the paper out in front of him, cleared his throat and read once more: "*I will go at night by candlelight. I will use the passageway*

behind the upper gallery and be back before he
notices I am gone."

"That's how Bunty knew about the passageway," Maximilian said. "She found it in the diary. She left the dinner to look for it. Then the next day she used it to sneak back in after she had been to the theatre to scare Sylvia and Agnes. That was why she came dashing down the stairs in such disarray. She must have crept back through the secret passage, thrown off the Viscountess's dress and run downstairs as Sylvia and Agnes came in from the lawn."

"If Bunty has been hiding the diary from her father, then she is the only person who actually knows where the missing diamonds are," said Oscar.

Maximilian did not answer. He had a glimpse of something in his mind's eye, a cascade of crescent moons down a frock, curving round in an elegant bow. Sylvia's frock.

"I think I know where they are!" he cried. "I

think Sylvia found them first. There were crescent-shaped jewels in the theatre. She thought they were just glass, so she has them sewn on to her evening dress for the party tonight!"

"But they must be priceless," gasped Oscar.

Maximilian nodded. He was no longer upset that Bunty might be involved. He was worried for Sylvia. If Bunty was prepared to scare the company away from the theatre to get her hands on the diamonds, what might she do if she realised Sylvia had found them?

"We have to find a way to warn Sylvia!" he cried.

CHAPTER 15
The Halloween Ball

They sped through the castle, sliding down stone banisters and taking the stairs three at a time. The Great Hall was packed with maids and footmen carrying trays of champagne glasses and being lectured by the stern-looking butler. The slippery marble floor stretched out before them. Maximilian gritted his teeth.

"Follow me!" he cried, and took a flying jump from the bottom step, landing on the smooth marble and throwing all of

his weight forwards. He skidded the length of the floor, leaning his weight to the right or left to steer round the legs of Lord Fawley's staff, spun in an arc round the feet of the butler and bounded out of the open front door. Oscar followed and together they ran across the lawns towards the theatre.

Inside the auditorium, the company was a-flurry with its final preparations. Miss Julier was working with the small orchestra that Lord Fawley had engaged to play for the evening's entertainment. Mrs Garland was dashing from one person to the next checking costumes for last-minute adjustments. Monsieur Lavroche had become so panicky that he had changed his waistcoat six times. Sylvia was nowhere to be seen.

Maximilian leapt up on to the stage and, nipping between the legs of some of the chorus who were stepping out one of the dances in the finale, he made his way towards Sylvia and

Agnes's dressing room. As he neared the door he could hear them laughing with Bunty and Arabella.

"A flame! How wonderful. It's very naughty of you to tell us though," Arabella was saying. "It's all meant to be a secret till midnight. Oh, but I'd seen the dress anyway so I suppose it can't be helped."

Maximilian slipped into the dressing room. Agnes was holding her flame dress up against herself and admiring herself in the mirror. Arabella and Bunty were sitting on comfortable chairs, drinking pink cocktails.

"And what about yours?" Arabella said to Sylvia. Sylvia smiled and reached for her moonlight costume.

"Don't show her!" miaowed Maximilian frantically, but Sylvia just leaned down and tickled his head. She shook the shimmering fabric out and held the dress so that the crescent-shaped stones at the shoulder and neck flashed in the

light. Arabella gasped. Bunty's eyes grew narrow and keen.

"Such beautiful stones," she murmured.

Sylvia nodded. "We found them in the theatre. We'll give them back afterwards, of course, but Lord Fawley kindly said we could borrow anything we liked. They're so pretty."

Maximilian beat his paw on Sylvia's leg, frantically miaowing, "Stop drawing attention to them. They are the stones from the famous lost Moonrise", but Sylvia simply pulled the dress out of the way of his claws and slipped it carefully on to a hanger. Arabella and Bunty stood up.

"We'll let you get on," Arabella said, setting her empty glass down on the table and smoothing her frock. "We've got to get ready for your lovely performance." She kissed the air beside Sylvia's cheek and then, taking Bunty by the arm, led her friend out of the dressing room. As they left, Bunty took one last look at the dress and a victorious smile stole across her face.

Maximilian dashed back out to Oscar, who had taken refuge under one of the theatre seats, the scrap of diary still in his mouth. As Bunty and Arabella swept past, Oscar shrank out of sight.

"She's seen the diamonds!" Maximilian blurted out, watching to make sure that Bunty left the building. "And she definitely recognised them. We were right, which means we can't let Sylvia or that frock out of our sight for a second."

For the rest of the afternoon, while Oscar stood guard over the dress, watching for Bunty at the window of the dressing room, Maximilian trailed Sylvia. He dashed from wing to wing across the back of the scenery, checking to see that Bunty had not crept into the theatre, and made rather a nuisance of himself following Sylvia round while she was rehearsing her solo dance. Miss Julier eventually threatened to throw him out if he did not stop getting under everyone's feet. Sometimes he wished that he could melt into the shadows like Oscar. Having such fluffy fur was not good when one wished to work undercover.

At seven on the dot he positioned himself at the door and watched as Lord Fawley's guests poured out of the castle and made for the theatre down pathways lit by pumpkin lanterns. Lord Fawley had wanted his guests to make the most of the party's theme and they had not disappointed him. Among the costumes and elaborate masks, Maximilian could see a mummy wrapped rather uncomfortably in bandages, a headless nobleman and at least six witches, their hats competing with one another in both size and width. There were the usual fairies and knights, of course, and one guest had dressed herself as Queen Elizabeth in a gown so large that Maximilian wondered how she would fit into a theatre seat. It would be most embarrassing, he thought, but he suspected that the Queen would be required to stand through the performance.

Maximilian scanned the crowd for Bunty. He could see Lord Fawley, leading the way, dressed in one of the suits of armour from the hall.

Beside him walked a girl in a sea-green dress
with a mermaid's tail for a hem and a glorious
mask of glittering scales.

It must be Arabella, thought Maximilian, spotting her glossy black hair behind the mask. As the crowd filled the lobby of the theatre, exclaiming with delight at all the detail of its features, Maximilian squeezed himself through the sea of legs, trying to catch a glimpse of Bunty, but with everyone wearing masks and talking at once it was impossible.

"Ladies and gentlemen!" Lord Fawley announced, clinking the side of a champagne glass till the chatter in the room died down. "Welcome to my little theatre." There were murmurs of charming dissent at the word "little" and Lord Fawley accepted the compliment. "We are honoured to have the company from London's Theatre Royal with us this evening," he continued. "I have commissioned a piece entirely in Arabella's honour and it is to be performed for one night only, here, tonight!"

There was a burst of applause and the chatter grew to a crescendo once more as Lord Fawley threw open the doors to the auditorium and the guests took their seats. All, that is, except Queen Elizabeth. Maximilian had been right and she had to stand. Lord Fawley led the mermaid to the spiral staircase that climbed up to one of the tiny boxes overhanging the stage. Maximilian slipped back behind the curtains. The lights were dimmed, the audience hushed and the show began.

Maximilian kept his eyes on the audience throughout the show, watching to see where Bunty was, but every time he thought he had spotted her there was something about the way the suspect moved that made him realise he was mistaken. The Egyptian queen was just a little too tall to be Bunty and the Venetian sailor just a little too short. If only they had searched her room for her costume when they had the chance.

Up in the tiny box above the stage, Arabella's mermaid mask twinkled in the lamplight as she leaned over the balustrade to get the best possible view of her show. From her reactions it was clear that she was having the most wonderful evening. She applauded Sylvia's ballet solo and wept at Agnes's beautiful singing, and at the end of the evening she was the first to rise to her feet and call for encore after encore of the grand finale.

Maximilian peeked his head out between the curtains that had closed after seemingly endless bows and curtseys. Lord Fawley's guests were filing out of their seats, congratulating him on a wonderful treat. The doors of the theatre's lobby had been thrown open and moonlight flooded in from the garden beyond, where an orchestra had struck up for the ball. Sylvia and Agnes rushed to their dressing room in a great hurry to get changed so that they would not miss a second of the fun. Maximilian followed. Oscar was curled up on the dressing table, his one good eye trained keenly on the door. As

Sylvia and Agnes began to get ready for the party, Maximilian and Oscar slipped out of the room. It would never do to be present while a lady was changing.

"I haven't seen Bunty all evening," Maximilian said. "She could be disguised as anything."

"I'll go and look for her among the guests," Oscar said. "Don't let Sylvia out of your sight."

As Oscar set off for the gardens, Maximilian returned to the dressing room.

Sylvia was sweeping her hair up into a diamanté clip that she had been given for her birthday. Agnes tried various styles before deciding to tuck her own bobbed curls behind her ears. They admired one another in the mirror, giggling over what a surprise they were going to give everyone in their new dresses.

"It's a shame we don't have a mask for Max," Sylvia said. "Maybe he could have some sparkle."

She blew glitter over his fur and Maximilian

shuddered. He did not approve of glitter. It was most undignified.

"Don't forget your mask," Sylvia said, tying her own feathered creation with ribbons behind her head. She grabbed Agnes's hand and they ran through the theatre to join the partygoers. Maximilian hurried after them, trying to shake the horror of the glitter from his tail.

CHAPTER 16
The Viscountess

Out in the garden, the party was in full swing. On the ornamental lake guests giggled as they trod the gangway up to the ghostly galleon and shrieked with joyful terror at the skeletal barmen serving cocktails with flavours like "Spooky Strawberry" and "Ghastly Gooseberry". A team of footmen had been set to work winching witches' hats up and down the wires that stretched from the windows of the castle to the ground, and in the great marquee that

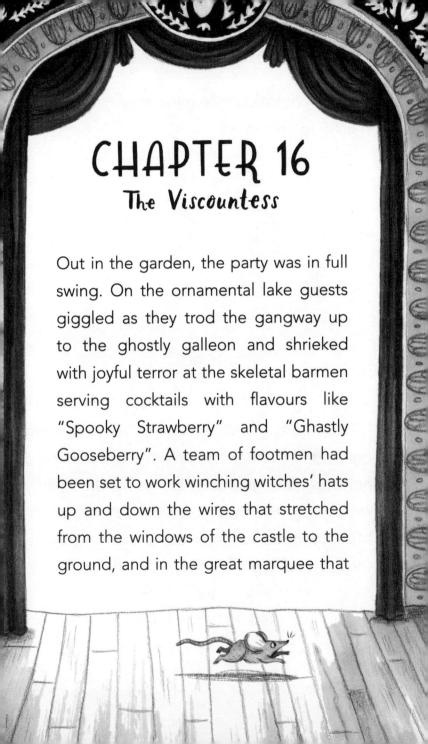

had been set up on the West Lawn, guests helped themselves to the very best that Lord Fawley's cook could provide. Maximilian's tummy gave a little groan at the sight of the enormous salmon that was laid out on one of the tables, but he gave himself a shake. He had to concentrate. Sylvia could be in great danger.

As Sylvia and Agnes tripped down one of the gravel paths towards the dancing, a masked waiter appeared from behind a hedge and passed them each a sparkling drink.

"How decadent," giggled Sylvia, reaching out for a glass. Maximilian peered at the waiter, then a dreadful thought struck him. The drinks could be drugged or, worse still, poisoned! Until Bunty was caught, Sylvia must not eat or drink anything. Before Sylvia could take one of the glasses, Maximilian sprang up and knocked the tray out of the waiter's hands.

Sylvia shrieked as the glasses smashed to the floor, soaking her dainty shoes. The waiter

leaned down to pick up the tray and the broken glass, scrabbling around to see through the narrow eyeholes cut in his mask.

"I can't see with this thing!" he exclaimed, whipping the mask away to reveal a handsome young man of about twenty. Mortified, Maximilian gave him his most polite "I'm terribly sorry, I mistook you for a dangerous miscreant" miaow but the man simply glared at him.

"Begging your pardons, ladies," the man continued, getting to his feet and bowing smartly to Sylvia. "There are plenty more drinks in the ballroom."

Sylvia apologised prettily for Maximilian's behaviour and ushered him ahead of her. A woman in a shimmering blue dress with peacock feathers pinned round the hem and wearing a towering peacock mask wandered past them, arm in arm with a soldier.

"I don't know what has got into Max," Sylvia said to Agnes. "He's been behaving a little oddly all week. Oh, my shoes are ruined, and they were brand new. Look what you've done, Max!"

But Maximilian was not listening. He had spotted something at the end of the lawn. From behind one of the bushes at the East Wing of the castle the figure of a woman in a long gown had appeared. Diamonds glinted in the dark hair tumbling in curls down her shoulders. As she passed one of the pumpkin lanterns on the stairs up to the castle, her gown twinkled with the light of hundreds of stars. It was the Viscountess. Bunty!

Leaving Sylvia dabbing at her dress with a napkin, Maximilian sped off after the figure in blue.

It took longer than usual to cross the lawn. There were people everywhere. Twice Maximilian had to leap over the long train of an unnecessarily elaborate dress, and once he had to take a large detour round someone dressed as a pumpkin. By the time he reached the castle he was very out of breath. He dashed into the hall. The Viscountess was standing like a statue in the middle of the floor, looking up towards her portrait. With the lamps turned down low so that the shadows flickered and danced and her dress shimmered in the half-light, there was something very eerie about it all. But Maximilian knew better than to believe all that nonsense about ghosts. This was Bunty, dressed as the Viscountess to scare everyone and steal the Viscountess's precious tiara from Arabella. Maximilian bounded across the floor and took a flying leap at her. As his claws sank into the soft velvet of her gown, the Viscountess flung her arms out either side and rose into the air. Maximilian yelped in horror as he felt himself soaring up and watched the marble of the hall sink away beneath him. What on earth was happening? He dug his claws in a little deeper, hoping that they would not give way. The Viscountess flew higher and higher, the great

cavern of the hall opening
up below, and Maximilian
started to whimper.

"Too high! Too high!
I faint if I am too high.
The vertigo!" cried the
Viscountess in a voice that
sounded suspiciously
familiar and not at
all Bunty-ish. She
waved frantically
at someone on
the ground and
then, with Maximilian
still clinging to her dress,
she sank back towards
the floor. When they
were about three cat-
lengths from the ground,
Maximilian loosened his
grip and fell, his paws

feeling very shaky.

"Honestly, I should have done it myself," said a voice from a shadowy alcove to the side of the hall. Lord Rorston stepped out, crossed to the Viscountess and tugged a thick wire from the back of her dress. She put a hand up to her head and, removing her wig, gave her head a good scratch. Maximilian gasped as the true identity of the Viscountess was revealed. It was Antonio.

"I hate this costume," he whined. "And this dress is covered in mud. Why should this be so?"

"You must have got it dirty when you were play-acting in the galleries the other night," said Lord Rorston. "What a fright you gave everyone, making it look like the Viscountess had escaped from her portrait. Very clever. You'll have to give the painting back at some point, though, old chap. It's terribly valuable, you know."

Antonio looked astonished. "Me?" he said. "You thought it was me? I was fast asleep in that ridiculously short bed that they have given me.

Such a silly bed, it would not fit a child. A tiny child. A mouse of a child—"

Lord Rorston cut him off. "But if it wasn't you pretending to be the Viscountess, who was it? I thought you were adding a little Halloween atmosphere."

Antonio fixed Lord Rorston with a steely glare. "I am the Great Furigo, the most accomplished illusionist in all of London. I *am* the atmosphere!"

Maximilian's head reeled. Furigo! Of course. *That* was why Antonio had seemed so familiar, and why he thought he remembered that peculiar hand movement the man had. This was the Great Furigo. But why was a magician here and pretending to be a researcher? In a moment, Furigo solved that mystery for him.

"Ah, the little cat fellow," said Furigo, spotting Maximilian. "You like our magic trick for Arabella, yes? We catch her a ghost for her party. It will be a great joke."

A joke? Maximilian felt his tail almost buzzing.

So Lord Rorston *had* been planning to scare everyone with the Viscountess's ghost, but as a joke. That was why he had invited Furigo to stay. Who better to create a ghost than a famous magician, and one who had astounded London by making a ghost appear on stage?

Bunty must have known about all of this, he thought. *She must have borrowed the dress without her father knowing, to perform her own hauntings. It was the perfect opportunity for her to scare us all away while she searched for the diamonds.*

Maximilian liked solving mysteries, but any satisfaction he may have felt on solving this one was short-lived. The blood drained from his head as he realised one more thing. While he had been chasing Lord Rorston and Antonio, Sylvia was out in the garden.

And so was Bunty.

CHAPTER 17
Sylvia in Danger

Maximilian dashed across the lawn to where he had left Agnes and Sylvia, but there was no sign of them. He looked around desperately, scanning the throng of party guests. He could see Lord Fawley talking to Queen Elizabeth by one of the fountains and a few metres away Arabella was holding court to the mummy and a couple of gondoliers. Maximilian swept his gaze across the party. Far across the lawn, by the entrance to the rose garden, there had been a flash of silver picked

out by the moonlight. Sylvia's dress!

He leapt down into the crowd and dodged between the feet of the partygoers miaowing his "please let me through, I am attempting a dangerous rescue" miaow. The night air was full of music and clinking champagne glasses. Maximilian leapt over one of the pumpkins lining the pathways, trying not to wince as the lantern inside it singed his tummy. A dark shadow fled towards him, one emerald orb flashing out in the dark. Oscar.

"The rose garden!" his friend panted. "I couldn't do anything. I'm sure it's Bunty."

Maximilian pushed on and reached the rose garden in a matter of moments. Ahead he could see Sylvia arm in arm with someone dressed as a milkmaid. He picked up the pace to catch up with them, all the time frantically miaowing at Sylvia to go back to the party.

"Lord Fawley asked if we could collect some of the roses for Arabella. Silly man, he forgot to sort it out earlier," the girl in the milkmaid's costume was saying. It was definitely Bunty's voice. As they turned a corner at one of the ornamental hedges, she slipped a hand into one of the folds of her dress and drew out a knife. Maximilian felt his heart leap with fear. He let out a roar and sprang, his teeth and claws flashing, and sank them into the girl's leg. Bunty shrieked and kicked out, trying to shake him off. He clung on. The girl twisted herself round and, with a vicious kick, slammed Maximilian into a stone urn. He fell to the ground. His head was spinning and his eyes blurred.

"Bunty!" Sylvia cried. "What on earth are you doing? It's Max!" She dropped to her knees and stroked Maximilian's head. He gave out a tiny miaow that was meant to say "never mind me, follow Oscar back to safety", but Sylvia did not understand. He was aware of Oscar beside him, hunkering down and hissing at Bunty, ready to attack.

"Stupid animal. I never did like cats!" Bunty spat. She leaned over Sylvia's shoulder and the moon glinted against the blade of the knife. Oscar leapt towards her and with a flash she had slashed at his leg, making him fall to the ground. Bunty grabbed at the shoulder of Sylvia's dress, twisting the fabric into a tight knot on which the Moonrise diamonds sparkled. Sylvia cried out as the blade pressed into her shoulder.

"I knew it!" Bunty said. "The minute I saw your dress I knew you had found them. You don't even know what they are, do you, you silly girl!"

"I ... I don't know what you mean!" Sylvia said, her eyes wide with fear.

"The Moonrise," Bunty said, pushing the blade more firmly against Sylvia's shoulder. "You sewed them into this ridiculous *thing*. They're worth a fortune! Well, you're not having them. They're mine! I did all the work in the family archives. Everyone thought the Moonrise had been sold, just like all the other jewels. Daddy loaned me the Viscountess's diary as something to read on the journey down here. He didn't want to be bothered with a silly girly diary. He was far too busy looking through dreary old estate papers, writing some silly history for Lord Fawley and plotting some stupid practical joke to give Arabella a ghost on her birthday. Because Arabella always has to have what she wants, doesn't she! Well, more fool him! I found out about the Viscountess and her hiding place. I discovered that the Moonrise was still here. It's mine!"

With a flash of the blade that made Sylvia shriek with terror Bunty tore the frill away from the front of Sylvia's gown. She stuffed it into her pocket and, turning on her heel, she ran from the garden.

Sylvia gasped. "Max, we must tell Lord Fawley," she said in a shaking voice. She scooped Maximilian up and cuddled him close, but he wriggled free. This was no time to wait for the humans. Bunty was going to get away with Arabella's diamonds and only Maximilian and Oscar could stop her. With a "follow me" miaow he dashed away after her.

CHAPTER 18
Bunty's Escape

Maximilian and Oscar ran through the gardens with Sylvia close on their heels. Bunty pushed her way roughly through the guests, colliding with a tall lady decked out in an elaborate eagle costume and getting tangled up with her plumed headdress. Tearing herself away, she ploughed on, knocking a tray of glasses out of a footman's hand and making a beeline for the side of the castle. Following her, Sylvia rounded the side of one of the fountains decked with

pumpkin lanterns and ran full pelt into Arabella.

"What on earth?" cried Arabella. "You almost spilled my drink."

"There's no time to explain," gasped Sylvia. "We have to catch Bunty. She has the diamonds."

Arabella's eyes grew wide. "What diamonds?"

"The Moonrise stones."

Arabella frowned. "What on earth are you talking about?"

Sylvia coughed and caught at her breath. "Bunty found them. Something about the Viscountess hiding the stones in the theatre. I had them sewn into my dress, but I thought they were just glass. She attacked me in the rose garden and stole them."

Maximilian miaowed in frustration. They were wasting too much time talking! He grabbed hold of the tail of Arabella's mermaid costume and tugged at it, miaowing his "hurry, she's getting away with the diamonds" miaow, and dashed off after Bunty. Sylvia grabbed Arabella's hand

and followed.

Maximilian and Oscar sprinted across the grass. In the middle of the beautifully tended lawn that spread out before them stood a tiny plane. Bunty was clambering into the cockpit and feverishly working at the controls.

"Lord Rorston's plane!" Maximilian cried. "So *that's* how she's planning to escape."

Maximilian dashed forwards, throwing every last bit of energy at reaching Bunty before she took off.

He reached the plane as it spluttered into life and began to trundle forwards, the wheels cutting deep grooves through the soft ground. Maximilian hunkered down, ready to pounce, then sprang at the passenger seat in front of Bunty. It was a narrow miss and he found himself hanging from the side of the plane as it swung violently round and Bunty prepared to roll down the lawn for take-off.

His paws scrabbling at the cold metal,

Maximilian clawed his way into the front. Bunty pushed down hard on one of the levers in the front of the cockpit and they started to pick up speed, careering towards Oscar and the girls.

He heard Sylvia shout "no!" and push Arabella
to the ground as the plane lifted itself into the
air and soared over their heads. In the control
seat Bunty laughed, a spiteful cackling laugh.

"And now to get rid of you!" she snarled, glaring down at Maximilian.

Suddenly they lurched to the side and Maximilian felt himself slipping on the leather seating as it tilted towards the ground. He dug his claws in and let out a frightened "mrowwww". The girl was trying to tip him out! One of the taller trees on the estate loomed up in front of them and Bunty swung the plane back at the last minute, the edge of the wing just clipping it and sending branches tumbling to the ground.

Maximilian sprang on to Bunty's lap and slipped down into the cockpit. The girl swiped at him but she could not grab at Maximilian *and* control the plane at the same time. Instead, she grasped the steering stick still tighter and pulled, tipping once more towards the ground. Maximilian slid sideways. Below, he could see the ghostly galleon being cut free from its moorings and sent off into the middle of the ornamental lake, where it would form the centrepiece for a grand firework display at midnight. He saw Sylvia and Arabella running through the gardens to where the guests danced, oblivious to the drama unfolding above their heads. And he saw the ground, frighteningly far away and not looking like a soft landing place for a small cat.

"Get out!" hissed Bunty, kicking at Maximilian. Maximilian hissed back at her. The girl's knuckles were white with the pressure of pulling on the steering stick. The plane tipped further to the side. Soon Maximilian would be rolled out altogether.

With a miaow of "you cannot get away with this", Maximilian wrapped his magnificent tail around the stick and pulled as hard as he could. The plane swung back suddenly, jolting Maximilian over to the side. Bunty cried out with anger but it was too late – the plane had swung out of control. There was an awful splutter and the propeller on the front stopped spinning.

"No!!!" screamed Bunty. She scrabbled

desperately at the controls, but the plane started to free-fall down towards the ground. Maximilian miaowed in terror as the lake reared up to meet them. He saw the water gleaming in the moonlight, the party guests gathering for the firework display and, straight ahead, cobwebbed and glowing under its hundreds of lanterns, the ghostly galleon.

The plane sank lower and lower, one wing skimming the water as it tipped to the side. Then, at the last minute, Maximilian sprang at the steering stick, landing on it with his full weight, and the plane veered sharply to the left. It hit the lake with a splash that made the galleon buck out of the water, rattling its sails and shaking the cobwebs from the rigging. The plane sliced through the water, spinning to a stop in the middle of the lake, where it started to sink.

Bunty clambered out of the cockpit, her face a mask of fury, and tumbled into the lake.

Maximilian splashed his paws about in alarm. The lake water was freezing and foul-tasting, and the cockpit was quickly filling with it. There was nothing for it; he was going to have to swim. He hauled himself out of the cockpit and flopped over the side in a most undignified manner, letting out a "mrow!" of surprise as the ice-cold water coursed over his fur. Maximilian paddled with his paws, but the water flooded into his mouth and ears, making him gasp and choke, and before he had moved forwards even one cat-length he felt his bottom sinking into the water. He kicked out with his back legs and, little by little, edged towards the bank. Ahead of him he saw Bunty, She was struggling, her arms flailing around. As he drew near her, her head disappeared under the water. She pushed herself up, spluttering.

"My dress!" she shrieked. "It's too heavy!"

She sank below again. Maximilian ducked his head down under the water, ignoring the cold as it rushed into his ears. Pushing as hard as he could with his back legs, he dived down towards Bunty. The great folds of fabric around the waist of her milkmaid dress were tied on with ribbons at the back. If he could only unleash them, then she could swim to the surface again.

Maximilian pushed himself down, feeling his lungs tighten. Reaching the girl, he clawed at the ribbons on the back of her gown. His lungs began to burn and he was desperate to breathe again. His head swam and he could feel his paws growing weak. He was about to pass out when his claw whipped one of the ribbons free and the folds of fabric around Bunty's dress fell away down into the lake. Freed from the weight, Bunty kicked up towards the surface, taking Maximilian with her.

Maximilian surfaced, gasping for air. Through the water in his ears and fur he heard muffled shouts of men dragging the frantic Bunty on to the lawn. One grabbed Maximilian by the scruff of the neck and deposited him by the side of the lake, where Sylvia fell on him, rubbing him down with the fabric of her shawl to get him dry.

CHAPTER 19
The Final Clue

They were all gathered in Lord Fawley's wonderful library. Bunty was wrapped in a thick woollen blanket, and a huge fire crackled in the grate. Lord Rorston stood by his daughter, running his hands through his hair and looking utterly distraught.

Maximilian was being dried off rather too roughly by one of the maids. He could feel his fur being pulled into all sorts of directions and was sure that he was going to look a sight by the time she

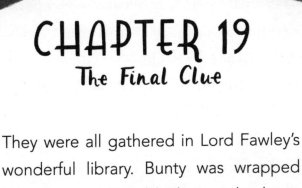

had finished.

"And this magnificent cat really knew that you were in danger, my dear?" Lord Fawley was saying to Sylvia.

Sylvia nodded. "Oh yes. Max is a genius. He has a real nose for mystery."

Lord Fawley murmured "quite wonderful" under his breath. Maximilian tried to look as noble as it was possible to look when one's hair is sticking out at all angles.

"So the Moonrise was hidden in the theatre all these years," said Arabella. "What a shame it's probably at the bottom of our lake. Still, no one got hurt. That's the main thing." She looked across at Bunty as she said this and it was clear to Maximilian that someone *had* got hurt. Arabella had lost her best friend.

"Why did you do it?" she asked, her voice breaking a little.

The girl had been staring wordlessly at the fire, refusing all attempts by her father to get her to drink some hot, sweet tea or eat a little cake. She stirred and glared at Arabella.

"Why should you always have the nice things?" she snapped. "Do you know why Daddy *really* agreed to do this silly archive work for your father? It was because we need the money. We've been selling everything. The pearl necklace Mummy left for me, our car. We only still have the plane because no one wants to buy it. No one had seen your tiara in years. No one would miss it. Why shouldn't I keep it? It was me that found it! It was all there in the Viscountess's diary. She didn't go over to the theatre to burn the silly thing down. She went to hide her diamonds so no one would find them. Well, I found them!"

A tear ran down Arabella's cheek. "Oh, Bunts," she sobbed. "Why didn't you just ask for help?"

Maximilian watched Bunty. In the garden she had been so vicious and cruel, but now she seemed like a frightened young girl. He could

179

still see the flash of the blade as she pressed the knife against Sylvia's neck and feel the pain of being thrown against the floor, but in spite of everything he felt a little sorry for her.

Lord Fawley put a hand on Lord Rorston's shoulder. "We'll do our best for her, Rorston," he said. "I'm sure we can keep all this out of the papers. We've been friends for years, after all. If we can just recover the portrait..."

Maximilian gave his "nothing could be simpler" miaow and dashed from the room. It took him a while to get up to the first floor and back, dragging the heavy canvas behind him. While he made his way across the Great Hall he was sure that he heard cries above him, but he shook the thought away as just nonsense. When they were back in London he would be very happy never to hear the word "ghost" again.

When he got back to the library, Lord Rorston was pulling a coat on to Bunty, and Lord Fawley was directing one of his footmen to drive them to a hotel in the nearest town. Maximilian dragged the painting to the middle of the room and nudged it with his nose to unroll it.

"Max, you marvel!" Sylvia exclaimed as everyone stared at the Viscountess's portrait spread out on the library floor. "Where was it? Oh, how I wish you could talk."

Max decided that this was not the time to point out that he *could* talk and that the problem was that Sylvia could not understand him. Instead, he glared very pointedly at Bunty. The girl buttoned up the coat and pushed a lank piece of hair out of her face.

"It was in my room," she said sullenly. "I didn't damage it, if that's what you're all thinking."

Lord Rorston shook his head sadly.

"I feel very responsible," he said. "The girls tell me that Bunty learned of the tiara in the Viscountess's diary. If I'd done my job properly and read the diary myself instead of letting her read it, it would have been me who stumbled across the truth about the diamonds, not Bunty, poor girl."

The mention of the diary reminded Maximilian of Oscar. Did he still have the page that revealed where the jewels were hidden? And was he safe after Bunty had hurt his paw so badly? Max glanced up to one of the windows, where he thought Oscar might be hiding, but there was no sign of him. As he looked back to Sylvia, who was patting Arabella's hand, his attention was drawn to a movement behind one of the curtains draped across the long room to keep the draughts out. A black face peered round and Oscar stepped into the library. At first, Maximilian thought that he was carrying the scrap of the diary, but then there was a flash in the lamplight and he realised that Oscar was carrying something else altogether. He walked across the room towards Arabella, limping a little from the wound on his leg. He was dripping wet, his sleek black fur bedraggled and sopping. When he reached Arabella he dropped the scrap in her lap, making her recoil a little at how wet it was.

Then Sylvia saw what Oscar had brought them.

"That's from my dress," she cried. "It's the diamonds!" Arabella's face lit up and she smoothed the fabric across her lap, marvelling at how the stones made the light dance around the room.

"Is this one of your cats too?" asked Lord Fawley.

Mrs Garland shook her head. "He looks oddly familiar, but no, he's not ours," she said.

Maximilian placed himself next to Oscar and miaowed his "this is my best friend, Oscar, and I couldn't have solved this crime without him" miaow.

"Well, Max likes him, so that's good enough for us," said Sylvia.

"And he rescued my diamonds," declared Arabella.

"Don't forget Max's contribution," said Sylvia. "He found where Bunty had hidden the portrait – that must be why he came after Bunty when she took me into the rose garden. He *knew* she was up to no good."

"And he rescued you," said Agnes. "And he fished Bunty out of the lake, even though she didn't really deserve it. He's a marvel, he really is."

"It was you dressing up as Lady Celine, wasn't it?" Sylvia said, eyeing Bunty keenly. "Were you trying to frighten us away from the theatre so you could hunt for the diamonds?" Bunty did not meet Sylvia's gaze.

"I wonder if Max knew that it was really Bunty dressing up, not a ghost," Agnes said.

Maximilian miaowed his "of course I did" miaow, but he was drowned out by Lord Rorston giving out a shout of alarm.

"The ghost! Oh my goodness, Antonio!" he cried. "We were in the middle of rehearsing a surprise for you at midnight, my dear, and I completely forgot about him."

The rest of the room looked after Lord Rorston in confusion as he dashed out to rescue the Great Furigo from the ceiling of the Great Hall.

"You did it again, Maximilian," Oscar said as they walked together down to the lake for the firework display. The rest of the guests hardly seemed to have missed their host and hostess. They had been enjoying the fire jugglers and the orchestra and the wonderful cocktail bar. Everyone had lost track of time and there was much delight when Lord Fawley announced that it was almost time to take their masks off.

Maximilian smiled. "We did it again. We almost made a terrible mistake and accused the wrong person, but we worked it out in the end."

"And still a night of party-going to enjoy," said Oscar. "I think we might have earned some of that salmon now, don't you?"

Maximilian grinned and the two friends turned to head for the marquee, but Maximilian felt himself lifted into the air.

"No so fast, Max," Sylvia laughed. "We have a surprise for you."

"You too, puss," said Agnes, hauling a horrified Oscar into her arms. Maximilian stifled a laugh. He was used to being snatched up by the humans but Oscar looked most affronted.

At the side of the lake, Lord Fawley stood with his arm round Arabella. The crowd of party guests waited politely, expecting a speech from their host. As Sylvia and Agnes arrived, Lord Fawley reached for a champagne glass from a footman waiting nearby.

"Ladies and gentlemen, tonight a precious family heirloom has been restored to us. I cannot go into the details, but the thanks for this fortunate event are due entirely to these two splendid cats, Maximilian and his friend ... erm..."

He looked at Agnes, but she only shrugged. "We don't know his name, sorry."

"Well, I give you a toast to Maximilian and friend," finished Lord Fawley.

"To Maximilian and friend," repeated the party guests, a little taken aback. They had never been called upon to toast a cat before.

Maximilian looked across at Oscar and raised a paw in toast to him. "To Oscar," he said. "A true friend."

"Likewise," replied Oscar.

The guests drained their glasses and turned to watch as the fireworks on the lake were lit and the sky above Fawley Castle exploded with colour and sound.

CHAPTER 20
The Next Adventure

"Where's your friend, Max?" Sylvia said, loading her case into the car that would take her and Agnes back to London. They had all slept rather late after the party, and the company hadn't begun to pack their costumes and props into boxes until almost noon. Sylvia bundled Maximilian into the seat next to Agnes, who was lazing in the back, her head lolling on a pillow.

Maximilian miaowed his "but we can't go without Oscar" miaow and heard an

answering miaow from the inside of the car. A dark shadow in the corner uncurled itself and a green eye winked at him.

Sylvia looked back at the house and waved at Arabella, who came over to say goodbye.

"Are you super excited?" she asked. "I'd be over the moon if it were me. Papa is always promising we'll go but somehow we never get round to it."

Sylvia stared at her. "Excited about what?" she said.

Arabella gasped. "Oh gosh," she said. "I hope I haven't let the cat out of the bag."

Maximilian let out his "we don't use that expression, it isn't polite" miaow but Arabella did not notice. Instead, she turned and called to Lord Fawley.

"Papa, is the trip meant to be a surprise? I think I've just given the game away."

They were joined by Lord Fawley and Monsieur Lavroche.

"Well, you may as well know," Monsieur Lavroche said. "We have had an invitation from an old friend to join her in Paris this spring."

Agnes's eyes grew as round as saucers. "Paris!" she breathed. "Oh, how romantic. Will we see the Eiffel Tower?"

Monsieur Lavroche nodded. "I'm sure there will be time for a little sightseeing. I myself intend to visit some of my family while I am there, and I'm sure our hostess will want to show us round her beautiful city."

Sylvia's brow puckered. "Someone we know who lives in France," she murmured.

"Madame Emerald!" miaowed Maximilian.

"Madame Emerald," said Monsieur Lavroche at the same time. "She wishes to see you all again very much."

"Madame Emerald the singer?" Arabella asked, sounding most impressed.

"She's Max's biggest fan," Sylvia said. "He rescued her from a kidnapper last year and

foiled an imposter who was impersonating her.
I'm sure she's going to make a huge fuss of him.
He'll come back from Paris even more conceited
than he is already, won't you, Max!"

Arabella leaned into the car and stroked
Maximilian's head. "He's wonderful," she said.
"You're so lucky to have him."

"We are," Sylvia agreed. "He's the cleverest
cat in the world. We would never have realised
what Bunty was up to without him."

As they pulled out of the castle gates Agnes
said, "There's one thing we never did solve.
How on earth did Bunty manage to make herself
disappear that night in the gallery when she was
dressed up as the Viscountess?"

Sylvia puzzled over this. "Any ideas, Max, old
thing?" she said, nuzzling Maximilian's head.
"I'll bet you and your clever friend have solved
that one too."

Maximilian looked at Oscar, but he only
shrugged. "Sorry, old friend, but it was the

diamonds or the diary when I jumped into that lake. I thought Arabella would prefer her jewels so I dropped the diary and when I got out of the lake it had blown away. The Viscountess's secret passageway will just have to remain a secret, unless Bunty ever tells, of course. I wonder if they'll ever work out how it was done,"

"Possibly," said Maximilian. "The humans aren't always as unintelligent as we think. Not as clever as us cats, of course. We solved another mystery. We're becoming quite good at this."

"And a Paris trip to look forward to," said Oscar. "Did I ever tell you about the last time I was in Paris…"

Maximilian smiled. He doubted that Oscar had ever been to Paris in his life, but he settled back in the seat and listened to his good friend tell another wonderful story as the car picked up speed on the open roads and carried them away to whatever adventure awaited them next.

THE END

DRAMATIS PERSONAE

The *Dramatis Personae* was just a fancy way of saying "cast list" in old theatre programmes. They were included so that all the people who helped put the show on could be seen as the fabulous people they were. So here is the list of important people who helped bring Max and Oscar's latest adventure to you. Please join me in giving them a big round of applause.

The Extraordinarily Excellent Editors
Kirsty Stansfield and Fiona Scoble, thank you for taking what I give you and showing me how to make it the best it can be. Thank you for making editing one of the most fun parts of the journey and for the encouraging comments in the margins that make me smile.

The Dazzling Designers
Nicola Theobald and Elisabetta Barbazza, thank you for making Max look his absolute best and for covers that make me cheer with delight.

The Amazing Agent
Joanna Moult, thank you for championing Max and cheering me on and always being there with great advice and endless support.

The Astounding Artist
Nicola Kinnear, thank you bringing Max to life with your incredible pictures. They are always perfect and I love them all.

The Fantastic Friends
My gorgeous Prime-Writers, thank you to the best writing group in the world. Thank you to everyone who worked through puzzles and mysteries with me over scones. Thank you to Rebecca Mascull for talking me through how an early twentieth century plane would work (all errors are entirely mine). Thank you to Debbie Moon for taking me round stately homes and listening to me talk about this series seemingly endlessly.

The Brilliant Booksquads
Booksellers, book bloggers and teachers who have read Max and shared him with readers, thank you from the bottom of my heart for all you do. A special tail-whisk from Max to all of you.

The Fabulous Family
Liz (this one's for you, remember all those ghostly movies we would watch together), Mum, Pete, Rick and Seren, I love you all.

The Heroic Husband
Neil, thank you for so many cups of tea, for endless encouragement and for just being amazing.
Love you. xxx

**So there are my important people.
Take a bow, everyone. You are all incredible
and this book would not exist without you.**

Sarah xx

LOOK OUT FOR:

MAX
The
DETECTIVE CAT

The
CATNAP
CAPER

In which our fearless
feline friend takes on a
Parisian mystery…